Louis Weber, C.E.O.
Publications International, Ltd.
7373 North Cicero Avenue
Lincolnwood, Illinois 60712

www.pubint.com

Manufactured in China.

8 7 6 5 4 3 2 1

ISBN: 0-7853-4261-3

Little
Life Lessons

Illustrated by Lance Raichert

Publications International, Ltd.

Contents

Contents

Pup Tent Pals

Written by Brian Conway

Puppy cannot wait to get home and start packing. His friends have planned a camping trip in the woods. This will be Puppy's first night away from home!

Puppy stuffs his backpack with everything he will need. He fills his canteen with enough water for everyone. Puppy's new sleeping bag is sure to keep him cozy warm inside his brand new pup tent.

Puppy meets the others at the edge of the woods.

"Did you bring the water?" asks Cat.

"It's right here in my backpack," Puppy replies. "Who has the marshmallows?"

"I have nothing but marshmallows in my pack!" says Hippo. "We should have enough to treat ourselves and any other campers we meet!"

"Other campers!" Turtle says. "Where we're going, there won't be anyone else around."

As the friends take the forest trail to their campsite, they talk about how much fun they will have camping.

Before it gets dark, the friends set up their campsite. Hippo and Bear gather sticks to get a campfire started.

Pig gets his tent ready first, but Puppy finds that he needs help. All tangled and toppling, Puppy's new pup tent almost gets the best of him, but Pig is happy to help. When they are done, it is already time for dinner.

"I thought we'd have a snack before dinner!" Hippo calls. The friends get together around the campfire. They toast marshmallows on a stick until their supper is ready. Then they have more marshmallows for dessert!

Puppy passes the canteen around the campfire. "This is the best!" says Puppy. "At home we never get to have dessert before and after dinner!"

After the sun goes down, with only the moonlight and the light of their little campfire keeping their campsite bright, Cat starts to tell a spooky story.

Huddled in the dark woods around the campfire, Cat tells her friends about a ghost who lives in an old weeping willow tree.

The lonely ghost cries through the night. After everyone is asleep, the ghost flies from campsite to campsite. They all listen to Cat's spooky story with great interest. They want to know why the ghost is crying. That is the silly ending to Cat's scary story.

"Wooo-hoo, wooo-hoo," Cat howls in her most ghostly voice. "Wooo-hoo will share their marshmallows with a hungry ghost?"

The friends laugh. Everybody loves Cat's campfire story. Everyone except Hippo. "Ooo, I ate too many marshmallows," says Hippo. "I'll leave what's left for your ghost, Cat. Now it's time for me to go to sleep."

"It is getting late," Puppy agrees. "And I can't wait to try my new sleeping bag!"

"Bring it out here with us," say Pig and Turtle. "We're sleeping under the stars!"

"That sounds like an adventure!" says Puppy. After everyone is safely zipped up in their sleeping bags, Puppy turns out the little lantern.

Pup Tent Pals

As the flames of the campfire go down to a glow, the campsite gets a little chilly. Puppy never knew how very dark the woods get at night! Puppy is used to sleeping with a little night-light beside his bed. He wishes he had left the lantern on.

Puppy snuggles deeper into his sleeping bag. He likes being away from home. He also likes being outside, with nothing but the sky and the stars over his head. But he still cannot sleep. Puppy decides to count the bright stars in the sky until he falls asleep.

While Puppy counts carefully, one of the stars moves and another one disappears! Puppy rubs his eyes and keeps counting. One of the stars flashes on and off again.

Maybe Puppy does not like those silly stars much after all. They are playing tricks on his sleepy eyes!

Puppy thinks he might like the tent better. Still wrapped up in his sleeping bag, Puppy wiggles over to his pup tent, where Mouse and Bear are already sleeping soundly.

Puppy feels much better inside the tent. With Bear and Mouse there and a little roof over his head, Puppy feels warm and safe.

But it is much darker inside the tent. Puppy cannot even tell if his eyes are open or closed! He crawls out to get the lantern, just to keep it beside him in case he needs it.

With nothing but darkness around him, Puppy is still not sleepy. His little ears perk up every time he hears the campfire crackle or the dry leaves rustle.

Puppy's ears hear a new sound in the woods around their campsite.

"Whoooosh, kee-kee-eek," the sounds swirl around, and then they are gone.

"Whoooosh, kee-kee-eek," Puppy hears them again.

"Who's there?" Puppy whispers. He reaches for the lantern, but all he sees are Mouse and Bear, who are not stirring at all.

Puppy is beginning to wish he were at home, where the only creepy sounds come from his creaky old bed.

Puppy waits for the sound to go away. He tucks his head inside his sleeping bag.

Just when he thinks he might fall asleep, Puppy hears it again, "Whoooosh, kee-kee-eek."

Puppy wonders why his friends do not hear the creepy, creaky whistling sound.

"It must be because they are asleep," he whispers to himself. "I should be, too!"

Puppy decides to forget all about the sounds in the woods. He feels silly for getting so scared. He does not want his first night away from home to be scary. He wants it to be fun!

Puppy hums a little tune to himself. Sometimes that helps him fall asleep. But when he stops humming, Puppy hears a different sound. This sound is not out in the woods. It is right there on their campsite! Something is rumbling and grumbling around their tents!

Puppy peeks out. The flashing lights he saw in the sky are now flashing around the campfire!

Puppy hears another grumble and another rumble. He lets out a yelp and dashes back into his sleeping bag to hide. Mouse and Bear start to stir.

"What happened?" whispers Mouse.

"Did something out there scare you, Puppy?" asks Bear.

"There's something growling around the campsite," Puppy whimpers from inside his sleeping bag.

Bear listens carefully for a moment, then Mouse chuckles. "Hippo always snores when he's had too much dessert," she laughs.

Puppy pokes his head out to see. Sure enough, Hippo is snoring. But the scary lights still hover over the fire.

"What about those flashing lights?" Puppy asks.

"Haven't you ever heard of lightning bugs?" Bear giggles.

"They light up," Mouse explains.

"They live here in the woods, and they like to play around a campfire," adds Bear.

Puppy feels very silly. He turns the lantern off and climbs back into his sleeping bag.

Before they fall back to sleep, Bear and Mouse check on Puppy. "Will you be okay?" they ask.

Embarrassed, Puppy just nods his head. Mouse and Bear settle back into their sleeping bags. Except for Hippo's snores, the campsite is quiet again.

But Puppy's ears are still very alert. He hears the same creaky whistle he heard before. "Whoooosh, kee-kee-eek!"

"Did you hear that creepy howl?" Puppy whispers to Bear. "And what about those creaky squeaks?"

"Those are just forest sounds," says Bear. "C'mon, I'll show you."

Bear gets his flashlight from his pack. He leads Puppy out among the trees around the campsite. Bear points the flashlight high into the trees.

"Every time the wind blows through their branches, the trees make a whistling sound," Bear explains.

Next Bear points the flashlight into the bushes. "Here are your creepy creakers," says Bear, pointing to a family of friendly crickets.

Back in the tent, Puppy wraps himself inside his sleeping bag. He apologizes for keeping his friends awake. Mouse and Bear are very understanding.

"This is your first night away from home," says Mouse.

"And there are always new sounds in new places," says Bear.

Bear leaves his flashlight on for Puppy. Puppy likes to have a little light beside him, but he does not think he will need it now. His friends are there with him.

"I'm not frightened anymore," he tells his pup tent pals. "I just feel sleepy now."

Puppy listens calmly to the many forest sounds. Now that he knows where the sounds are coming from, sleeping outside is easy. The sounds go together to make a soft forest tune.

The wind whistles through the trees, and the crickets chirp to each other. Hippo lets out a snore that rumbles through the campsite. And before long, Puppy adds his own little snore to the gentle forest songs.

The New Kid

Written by Sarah Toast

It is almost time for morning recess in Ms. Hen's busy classroom. They have spent the morning reading, writing, and learning new spelling words.

The students are sitting quietly, waiting to be dismissed. It is a sunny day, and Puppy has stared out the window many times this morning.

Puppy sits up straight and looks like he is paying attention, but he is really thinking about what fun it will be to play tag with his friends at recess. Bunny is thinking up a new dance she wants to try out on the playground.

Pig wants to try a daring new trick on the jungle gym. Mouse hopes to play hide-and-seek. It is her favorite game to play at recess. There are lots of good hiding spots on the playground.

When everyone has stopped fidgeting, Ms. Hen says, "All right, class. You may walk in a line quietly down the hall and go out to recess. Enjoy yourselves! I'll be out in a few minutes."

Puppy leads the small parade quietly down the long hall. As soon as the students go out the big doors to the playground, they start to run and shout and play.

Bunny does a lively dance. "I like to call this dance Playground Polka," she says.

"That's a nice dance," says Puppy, as he happily runs around Bunny.

Mouse wants to play hide-and-seek. She skitters over to a new hole under a bush. She runs into the hole. Then she pops out and shouts, "Surprise!"

"Look at me!" shouts Pig. He is hanging by his knees from the high bars of the jungle gym and swinging back and forth. "Look at . . . oomph!"

Poor Pig has fallen from the bars. Bunny and Puppy run over to see if he is all right.

"That was part of my trick," says Pig, who is a little out of breath. "Do you want to see me do it again?"

"Sure!" shouts Bunny.

Pig is happy to perform for an audience.

Little Life Lessons

Puppy, Bunny, Mouse, and Pig are so busy playing that they do not see the new student who goes by himself into the school. The new kid is Skunk.

Skunk watches all the friends play. He hopes that they will like him. Skunk really wants to make new friends at his new school.

Skunk looks at the note in his hand. It has "3" written on it. He finds the door with a number three on it, then opens the door to Ms. Hen's classroom.

Ms. Hen is on her way to watch her students on the playground. As she leaves the classroom, she finds Skunk standing outside, peering through the open door.

"My goodness! My, my!" clucks Ms. Hen. "If it isn't the new student! We were just about to get ready for you! There is your new desk, Skunk, next to Puppy's desk. Over there is the cubby for your lunch box."

Skunk looks all around the bright classroom and smiles shyly. He likes what he sees. Ms. Hen makes him feel like he is welcome.

"Where are the other kids?" asks Skunk in a whisper.

"The students are at recess," says Ms. Hen. Then she adds, "Why don't you go on out to the playground and join them for the rest of recess. I'll get your desk set up with books, pencils, paper, and scissors."

Suddenly Skunk feels very shy indeed. He walks slowly down the long hall and pushes open the big door to the playground. Skunk sees all the students playing, but he just does not know how to join in.

Skunk is relieved that no one notices him. He stays close to the building as he walks toward the bushes at the edge of the playground.

When Skunk gets to the bushes, he sits down to watch the others play. The sunlight makes shadows in the bushes. With his bright white stripe on his back, Skunk is hard to see. He can watch the others play and still not be noticed.

He wonders if his new classmates will like him. Skunk is afraid that no one will want to play with him.

Skunk feels a funny tickle on the bottom of his foot. A moment later, he feels a sharp poke.

"Ouch," says Skunk as he lifts up his foot to rub it. Just then, Mouse scurries out of a hole that Skunk has not even really noticed.

Mouse gets a safe distance away from Skunk, then turns and says, "You scared me! You blocked the hole I was hiding in!"

"I didn't see the hole," says Skunk. "I was just sitting down to watch the kids play."

Mouse can tell that Skunk does not mean any harm, but still she is wary of this striped kid that she has never seen before.

"You know," says Mouse, "this playground is only for the students."

"Well," says Skunk shyly, "I'm new here. This is my first day of school. Ms. Hen told me to come out for recess."

"Well, why didn't you say so!" says Mouse. "I'll show you around!"

The New Kid

"Let's walk on over to the jungle gym, and I'll introduce you to Pig," Mouse says.

Skunk grins and heads over to the jungle gym. Pig sees a striped kid coming toward him, but he does not notice Mouse walking next to him.

For a second, Pig feels nervous. He considers jumping down and running over to Puppy, but then he thinks to himself, "Maybe this new kid appreciates talent."

"Hey, kid," Pig calls to Skunk. "You want to see the great trick I can do?"

"Sure!" says Skunk.

Pig swings back and forth by his knees.

"That is great!" says Skunk.

"Why don't you try it?" says Pig.

"Pig, this is Skunk, the new kid in school. I'm showing him around!" Mouse says.

Skunk climbs the bars, and he and Pig hang by their knees side by side. "Nice to have you here," says Pig.

Suddenly Bunny comes into view. She does a twirling leap and lands gracefully under the jungle gym — right under Pig and Skunk.

"Hello, down there!" say Pig and Skunk together.

Bunny curtsies and says, "Hello, Pig! I was dancing the Playground Polka."

Then Bunny looks up and jumps, but this jump is not part of her dance. Bunny jumps because she is startled to see the striped new kid.

Mouse comes to the rescue. "I don't think you've had a chance to meet the new kid, Skunk," says Mouse.

"Well, it's nice to meet you, Skunk," says Bunny, who feels a little bit shy herself. "Do you like dancing?"

"I don't know yet," says Skunk.

Pig and Skunk grab the bars and drop to the ground. Skunk takes two steps, does a long jump, and lands on both feet.

Skunk and Bunny laugh, and Mouse and Pig join in the laughter.

The New Kid

Puppy is dashing all over the playground, jumping over imaginary logs and puddles, when he hears his friends laughing. With a big smile on his face, Puppy runs up to his friends. He runs once around them before coming to a halt.

"Whew! That was fun!" says Puppy. "What are you laughing about?"

Mouse steps up and says importantly, "Puppy, we have a new kid at school. We'd all like you to meet Skunk."

With everyone looking at him, Skunk suddenly feels very shy again. He looks at the ground.

Puppy can tell that Skunk feels shy. Puppy walks up to Skunk and puts a friendly paw on his shoulder. "It's really great to have a new kid in the class," says Puppy.

"It sure is," says Mouse. "Especially one with such a neat-looking stripe!"

"Who appreciates talent!" says Pig.

"Who might like dancing!" says Bunny.

Skunk looks up and beams at his new classmates. "It's great to be here," he says.

"I have an idea!" says Puppy. "Let's think up a game we can all play together!"

"How about hide-and-seek?" says Mouse. She loves to hide in small places.

"How about a dance contest?" says Bunny, as she twirls on one foot.

"How about taking turns doing tricks on the bars?" says Pig.

"How about playing a game of tag?" says Puppy. "Then we can all run around together at the same time."

"Yes!" they all shout.

"I love to play tag," Skunk says to his new friends.

They all giggle and run around the playground. Skunk is beginning to feel like he fits in. He really likes all of his new friends.

Just then Ms. Hen comes out the big door to the playground and blows her whistle. The classmates all line up and march quietly into the classroom. Skunk walks next to Puppy and Mouse.

"Thank you for letting me play," Skunk whispers to Puppy.

"Why wouldn't we?" Puppy asks. "After all, you're part of our class now. That means you're our friend, too."

Mouse wants to finish the game of tag during their lunchtime recess. Puppy and the others agree.

Skunk is so happy to have new friends that include him in their fun. He can hardly wait until lunch.

The students quickly settle back into their seats. Ms. Hen smiles at her class and announces, "We have a new student. I'd like you to meet Skunk."

All the students smile at Skunk. Puppy quietly raises his hand.

"Yes, Puppy?" says Ms. Hen.

"Ms. Hen, we met Skunk out on the playground. We're all going to finish our game of tag at lunchtime recess."

Ms. Hen beams at her students. "Well done, class! And well done, Skunk! It's good to see that all of you became friends all by yourselves."

Everybody Cries

Written by Brian Conway

Puppy is having a very bad day, and it has only just begun. He has already missed his morning wake-up call. The birds usually come to his window to sing their wake-up song. Today Puppy did not hear them.

"Oh, my!" Puppy says. "I slept through the sunrise!"

Now Puppy must hurry if he wants to reach the bus stop on time.

Puppy does not have time to brush his fur. He quickly splashes some water on his sleepy face. If he takes the time to scrub behind his ears, he will surely miss the bus!

Puppy barely has time to get his books together and find his backpack! He digs through a pile in his bedroom.

"Where is my homework assignment?" he sighs.

Puppy likes to have a good breakfast before school. This morning he has no time for cereal, toast, or juice. He does not even have time to wait for the toaster!

Puppy grabs a dry biscuit from the kitchen counter as he leaves.

Everybody Cries

Puppy started his day in a hurry. He cannot slow down now. He runs from his house along the sidewalk. Bunny and Bear live on Puppy's block, but he is too late to meet them today.

Puppy zips around the corner. He is relieved to see the school bus still waiting at the end of the block. He cannot tell if the driver sees him, though.

Still running, Puppy sees Hippo climb aboard. Hippo is always the last one to make it to the bus stop. The driver always moves on after Hippo shows up.

"Wait for me!" Puppy shouts from down the block.

The driver has shut the door. All of Puppy's friends are busy talking on the bus and none of them hear him yelling. Nobody sees Puppy running and waving his arms either.

The bus pulls away just as Puppy reaches the bus stop. He is so out of breath and worn-out that he cannot run anymore. Puppy will have to walk to school today.

Puppy has never been late for school before. But he is very late today.

By the time Puppy gets to school, Ms. Hen has already started class.

Puppy sneaks through the door to Ms. Hen's classroom. He quietly shuffles to his desk.

Ms. Hen hears Puppy come in. She is writing on the blackboard and does not turn around to look at Puppy. But she does say good morning to him.

The other students giggle. Puppy is embarrassed. He shrinks down in his desk.

With a playful grin, Mouse nudges Puppy. "Thanks for showing up," she whispers.

Bear yawns a great big silly yawn. "You look tired, Puppy," he teases.

"I had to walk all the way to school today," Puppy whispers back.

Bear chuckles. "If you had taken the bus," he says, "maybe you wouldn't be so tired."

Ms. Hen asks the class to be quiet while she talks. Puppy cannot wait for this terrible morning to be over.

On the way to lunch, Puppy is very quiet. He thought his day would get better. But it is only getting worse!

"What's the matter, Puppy?" Cat asks kindly.

Puppy opens his backpack and looks in. "I forgot my lunch today," he sighs.

"That's okay," says Cat. "We'll all share our lunches with you."

Puppy's friends pass him bits from their lunches. Hippo shares his sandwich with Puppy. Bear gives him some crackers. Mouse shares her pudding. Cat gives him part of her apple.

"It's not the best lunch in the world," says Cat, "but it's better than no lunch."

Pig is the only one who does not share with Puppy. Pig eats so fast, there is nothing left to share! Puppy frowns at Pig, who hurries over to the swing set. Pig always wants to be the first one to get his favorite swing.

By the time Puppy finishes his lunch and makes it to the playground, all the swings are taken.

Puppy's sadness shows on his face.

"Sorry, Puppy," says Pig playfully. "You can have this swing when I'm done with it."

Puppy knows Pig is teasing him. Pig always stays on the swing until the bell rings.

Bear tells everyone about his news. Today he finds out if he made the baseball team!

"I think my chances are good," he says. "I had the most powerful swing in practice yesterday."

Bear shows his friends how good he is at baseball. While he pretends to catch, throw, and bat, Bear bumps into Pig's swing.

Pig falls to the ground and hurts his leg. He starts to cry. Mouse runs to help Pig, but Puppy laughs!

"Look at Pig," he says, "crying like a boo-boo baby!"

Pig's leg is only scraped, but Puppy's friends do not think it is funny. They are very surprised at Puppy!

After lunch Puppy goes back to his desk.

"It's time to turn in your homework," says Ms. Hen.

Everybody Cries

Everything has gone wrong today, but Puppy knows he remembered his homework assignment. He is sure he picked it up this morning, and he saw it in his backpack while he was looking for his lunch. Maybe his day is getting better after all.

Ms. Hen looks at every student's paper while she collects the assignments. She stops for a moment at Puppy's desk and looks at his paper. Puppy has a very bad feeling that he did not turn in the right assignment.

"I'm sorry, Puppy," she says, "but I'm afraid this is the wrong assignment."

Puppy shakes his head. He sighs a heavy sigh.

"And you were late for school, too," says Ms. Hen. "Is something the matter today?"

Puppy shakes his head again. "No, Ms. Hen," he says. "Everything is fine."

Everything is not fine today. Everything is just terrible! Puppy feels like crying, but he cannot do that now, not with everybody watching.

When the school bell rings, Bear is the first one out the door. He is in a hurry to get to the playground.

Puppy is the last one to leave his desk. He walks slowly to the door.

"Are you sure you are okay, Puppy?" asks Ms. Hen.

Puppy looks at Ms. Hen with sad eyes. "Sure," he says. "Everything is fine."

Puppy does not run out to the playground with the others. Cat sees him standing all alone. She knows that Puppy had a very bad day.

"Why don't you come with us?" she asks Puppy. "Don't you want to know if Bear made the team?"

"With the day I'm having," Puppy sighs, "I think I'd only bring bad luck to Bear."

"Don't be silly," says Cat. "Bear wants you to be there, to share his good news with him!"

"I think I'll wait and find out later," says Puppy, turning away. "I should go now. I don't want to miss the bus again today."

Puppy gets to the bus early. He is much too early to go home. The bus driver is not even there yet! Still, Puppy climbs aboard. He takes a seat in the back of the bus.

Puppy just wants a place where he can be alone. There on the bus, with no one around, Puppy thinks about his day.

He remembers all the bad things that happened. He got up late, forgot his homework, and teased Pig for crying on the playground.

There were so many times that he wanted to cry! But after he made fun of Pig for crying, he could not let any of his friends see him cry. Right now Puppy can think of many, many reasons to cry.

"Missed the bus, late for school," Puppy whispers sadly to himself.

"No breakfast, no lunch," he sobs.

"Wrong homework, wrong everything!" he sighs.

Puppy cannot hold back the tears. All at once, they pour from his eyes.

Before long, Pig joins Puppy on the bus. Puppy tries to wipe the tears from his eyes.

"Bear made the team!" he calls to Puppy. As he gets closer, Pig sees that Puppy has been crying.

"What's the matter, Puppy?" Pig asks kindly.

"All I wanted was a place to be alone," Puppy sobs. "But even that can't go right for me today!"

Pig is very concerned and sits down beside Puppy. He gently pats Puppy's shoulder.

"Everyone has a bad day once in a while," Pig says softly. "There's nothing wrong with crying sometimes."

Puppy cries some more. Between sobs and sniffs, he tells Pig he is sorry for being so mean on the playground.

Pig tells Puppy that his leg is much better now. He has forgotten all about it!

"The best thing about having the worst day ever," says Pig, "is that tomorrow will be a lot better. It has to be!"

After his talk with Pig, Puppy feels much better. For the first time all day, his frown changes to a smile.

Everybody Cries

When Bear and the others arrive, Puppy's tears are out of sight. He has a big smile for his friends!

They are all cheering for Bear. Bear's good news is the best news Puppy has heard all day.

"Congratulations, slugger!" Puppy happily says to Bear. "You made it!"

"My first game is tomorrow," says Bear. "I hope you can come to cheer me on."

"I'll be there!" says Puppy. "And I won't be late!"

His friends all laugh, and Puppy laughs for the first time all day.

Maybe his day is already getting better! Puppy thinks about what Pig said about tomorrow being a better day.

"I had so much bad luck today," Puppy tells Bear with a grin, "I'm pretty sure I'll bring you nothing but good luck tomorrow!"

They all laugh with Puppy. Seeing all of his friends reminds Puppy that even when he has a bad day, he is still lucky to have great friends.

Game Day

Written by Brian Conway

It is the end of the day at school, and Puppy and his friends cannot wait to get outside and play. Ms. Hen makes an announcement right before the bell rings.

"There will be no class tomorrow!" she says.

Everyone cheers!

"You mean we get to play outside all day long?" asks Skunk.

"You still have to come to school," Ms. Hen answers with a laugh. "But, yes, we'll be playing outside all day. It's Game Day!"

The students cheer again. Since Skunk is new to the class, he does not understand what all the excitement is about.

"Game Day happens once a year," Puppy explains. "We have contests out on the playground! It's like having recess all day long!"

Ms. Hen invites the students to sign up for their favorite Game Day events. Puppy and his friends rush to the bulletin board to get their names on the list.

Game Day

Hippo and Bear sign up for the tug-of-war again this year. They make a good team. Puppy and Bunny decide to try the three-legged race together.

"Who's going to sign up for the limbo contest?" asks Mouse. Mouse wins the limbo contest every year. Everyone knows she will have no trouble winning again this year. Bunny signs up anyway, just for fun.

At Game Day last year, Pig was the fastest in the sack race. "No one can beat me!" Pig says. Cat really wants to try, though.

Puppy does not see Skunk's name on the sign-up lists. Skunk is in no hurry to get his name on any of the lists.

"What's the matter, Skunk?" asks Puppy. "Don't you like contests?"

"I like games a lot," Skunk says shyly. "I'm just not very good at them."

"You should try the sack race," says Puppy. "I think you'll have fun!"

While the others rush out to the playground to start practicing, Skunk signs his name on the bulletin board. He puts his name next to Pig's on the list for the sack race.

Puppy and Bunny are already practicing for the three-legged race. They have never tried to run with three legs before! At first they topple and tumble with every step. Bunny cannot stop laughing! Soon they learn to take turns with their steps, and together they make a fast team.

Cat practices for the sack race, but Pig does not practice at all.

"I don't need any practice," says Pig. "And I'm still going to win by a mile!"

Skunk arrives on the playground. He sees Cat practicing with a sack and gets one for himself.

"So the new guy is going to try to beat me at the sack race, huh?" Pig says playfully. "Would you like me to give you a few pointers?"

Skunk smiles at Pig. But he is not looking forward to racing him on Game Day.

Game Day

The next morning on the playground, it is time for Game Day to begin. Ms. Hen gathers her students together.

"We must all remember to be good sports today," says Ms. Hen. "Don't forget to cheer for your friends!"

All smiles and ready to play, everybody cheers loudly.

"Okay, kids, if you're ready, let's go!" cheers Ms. Hen. "Let the games begin!"

They all hurry to the first event. Puppy looks back and sees Skunk moving slowly behind them. Skunk does not look like he is having fun.

"Come on, Skunk," says Puppy. "Aren't you ready for a great day?"

"I'm a little nervous," says Skunk. "I've never won a game in my life. I guess I don't want my new friends to think I'm a loser."

"You're not a loser, silly," says Puppy. "Everybody wins on Game Day. You'll see."

Skunk follows Puppy to watch the tug-of-war.

Before the tug-of-war starts, Ms. Hen reminds everybody that it does not matter who wins. The only thing that matters is that everybody has lots of fun!

Turtle and Cat hold one side of the rope, while Hippo and Bear hold the other.

Everybody cheers for Hippo, Bear, Turtle, and Cat. Hippo is big, and Bear is strong. They make a good pair for the tug-of-war.

The contest is over as soon as Ms. Hen shouts, "Go!" With one strong tug on the rope, Hippo and Bear pull Turtle and Cat down!

"Hooray for Hippo and Bear!" everyone cheers.

Even Turtle and Cat cheer for the winners. But Skunk does not cheer. He is still worried.

Puppy sees that his friend looks worried. He pats Skunk on the back. "That was a quick contest, wasn't it?" he says. "It was a lot of fun to watch."

Skunk is very worried. "I'm not strong," he whispers to Puppy. "I can't win."

Game Day

Puppy tries to cheer up his friend. "Just come and watch Bunny and me run the three-legged race," he says. "It'll be fun! And don't forget to cheer for us!"

The racers line up at the starting line.

"Get ready! Get set! Go!" Ms. Hen yells.

Puppy and Bunny are off and running! Their practice pays off. They move ahead of the other racers with every speedy step.

Hippo and Bear were much better at the tug-of-war. The clumsy pair tumbles and rolls across the playground! Even Skunk starts to giggle at the sight.

Skunk cheers for Puppy and Bunny when they cross the finish line.

Pig strolls over to Skunk. "Do you see that finish line? That's where I'll be after the sack race!" Pig says grinning at his friend.

When Puppy and Bunny come over to Skunk, he looks as worried as ever.

"I'm not fast," he sighs. "I can't win."

"Come and watch the limbo contest," says Puppy.

Bunny takes her turn first. She bends back to scoot under the low pole. She takes a few tiny steps before she slips backwards and drops into the grass. Her friends still clap and cheer.

"That is one dance step I need to practice," she laughs.

Mouse has been waiting all day for this event.

"Okay, everybody," she says. "Here comes the best little limbo of the day."

Mouse does a little wiggle dance at the limbo pole. With her friends clapping in time, Mouse sings a silly song:

> *Do you wonder, do you wonder,*
> *Can Miss Mouse go under?*
> *Don't you know, don't you know,*
> *I can go really low!*

The friends sing along and laugh. Mouse goes lower than anyone else could, and she puts on quite a show! Skunk is having so much fun with his friends that he forgets all his worries.

Game Day

Game Day

"It's time for the sack race!" Ms. Hen announces.

The smile on Skunk's face drops to a sad frown again. Puppy follows Skunk to the starting line. He watches Skunk climb clumsily into the sack.

Pig is the first one to get into his sack. He is the first one at the starting line, too.

"I'll see you at the finish line," he says to Skunk.

The friends cheer for Pig. They are sure he will win again this year. "Pig! Pig! Pig!" they chant.

Puppy comes over to talk to Skunk. "Isn't Game Day fun?" he asks. "Are you having a good time?"

"I don't want to lose this race," says Skunk. "I think I should just sink into this sack and never come out."

"Don't be silly," says Puppy. "The race is not important. If you have fun, you're a winner!"

Skunk thinks it over for a moment, and he smiles again. Before he knows it, Ms. Hen starts the race. "Get ready! Get set! Go!" she calls.

Pig gets off to a very good start. Everyone cheers, "Go, Pig! Go!"

But Skunk is fast, much faster than he thought he would be. Skunk hops ahead in his sack, springing across the playground.

"Look at Skunk!" Mouse shouts. "He is catching up!"

Then Skunk's friends start to cheer for him! "Go, Skunk! Go!" they call. "Go, Skunk! Go!"

Skunk springs past Pig, then Pig passes Skunk. They are racing side by side as they get closer to the finish line. It is the closest race of the day!

At the finish line, Pig makes a long leap to win the race, but just by a nose ahead of Skunk. Their friends cheer and clap for both racers.

"You ran a great race!" Skunk tells Pig.

Pig says, "So did you! Not bad for a new guy!"

Skunk is so happy! He can hardly believe that the race was so close. Not only did he almost win, but he had a lot of fun, too.

Skunk cannot wait to talk to Puppy about the race.

"Did you see me?" he says happily. "I almost won!"

"I saw you," says Puppy. "You looked like you were having fun!"

Ms. Hen calls her students to the playground. The games are over now. It is time to hand out the blue ribbons to all the winners.

"Anyone who won a contest," says Ms. Hen, "please raise your hand."

The winners raise their hands. Everybody claps and cheers for the winners.

Before Ms. Hen passes out the prizes, though, she adds, "Anyone who had fun, please raise your hand now."

Everyone in the group puts a hand up and cheers. Ms. Hen hands a big blue ribbon to each of her students. Skunk is surprised to have won a prize.

"It's what Game Day is all about," Puppy tells him. "When everyone has fun, we're all winners!"

The Lost Shoes

Written by Sarah Toast

One bright morning, Cat and Hippo are playing together in the park. It is Hippo's turn to push the merry-go-round to make it go fast. "Hang on tight!" says Hippo. "We're taking off!"

Hippo jumps up on the platform and hangs on with all his might as it spins around fast. Cat feels herself pulled toward the edge of the twirling merry-go-round. She hangs on as hard as she can, too.

As the merry-go-round begins to slow down, Bunny hops into view. Then she hops again, and yet again.

Bunny looks over at her spinning friends and bows. "I call this dance the Bunny Hop," she says proudly.

The merry-go-round comes to a stop. Cat thinks she feels a little bit queasy. She does not want to spin on the merry-go-round anymore. "Let's play with Bunny," she says to Hippo. "Let's all play tag!"

Hippo happily agrees. He loves playing tag with his friends in the park.

The three friends work up an appetite, running around playing tag. As much fun as it is to play, they are feeling hungry. They decide it is time to go home for lunch.

Hippo remembers he is supposed to meet Puppy for lunch. He yells good-bye to Bunny and Cat.

"I'll walk with you, Bunny," says Cat.

"Okay," says Bunny. They talk about dancing as they walk toward Bunny's house.

It is not long before Bunny begins to do more dancing than walking, because dancing is Bunny's favorite way to move. Cat laughs and skips along to keep up with Bunny.

Cat wishes she could dance like Bunny.

When Bunny and Cat get to Bunny's front porch, Cat says, "You dance so well, Bunny. I really would like to be able to dance like you."

"Thank you!" says Bunny, with a bow. "I really love to dance." She twirls around again and adds, "If you practiced you could dance, too."

Cat suddenly feels shy. "May I ask you a favor?" she says to Bunny.

"Well," says Bunny, "I guess so." Bunny is not sure what Cat wants, so she does not know if she will feel happy about doing Cat a favor.

"Would you let me borrow your dancing shoes for a few days?" asks Cat with a very sweet smile. "Your best dancing shoes? I want to learn how to dance! I think it would help a lot if I wore your dancing shoes."

Bunny hesitates. "I don't know, Cat," she says. "Whenever I dance in the house, I always wear my dancing shoes. I would hate to be without them."

"Oh, please, please!" says Cat. "I know your shoes will make me dance better!"

"But," says Bunny unhappily, "you don't always return the things you borrow."

"That's only because sometimes things get lost!" says Cat. "That's not my fault!"

Bunny takes a deep breath. "I hate to be the one to tell you this," she says, "but sometimes it is your fault when things get lost. If you would take good care of things, they might not get misplaced."

"I promise I'll take extra-good care of your dancing shoes! Will you just pretty please let me borrow them?" begs Cat.

Cat makes so many promises that Bunny finally lets her borrow the special shoes. Cat and Bunny go to Bunny's closet, where the dancing shoes are nestled in their shoebox on the floor.

"Don't wear these shoes outside," says Bunny. "They are only for indoors."

Cat is very happy. She tries to curtsy like a ballerina when she thanks Bunny.

"That was pretty good," says Bunny, and Cat is very pleased.

Cat heads home with the precious dancing shoes and a head full of dancing daydreams.

When Cat gets home, she puts the shoes carefully on her bed. Then she has her lunch.

As soon as Cat finishes her lunch, she takes her dishes to the sink and goes to her room to try on Bunny's best dancing shoes.

The shoes fit Cat very well. Cat puts on her favorite music. She dances, leaps, twirls, and bows all the way to dinnertime. After dinner, Cat practices some more.

Mouse comes over to play. "Come on in, Mouse," says Cat. "I'm practicing my dancing! I want to learn to dance like Bunny."

"Correct me if I'm wrong, but aren't those Bunny's dancing shoes?" asks Mouse.

"Yes, they are. Bunny let me borrow them," says Cat. Then she does a dance for Mouse.

Mouse is surprised Bunny let Cat borrow her shoes.

"I call this dance Catwalk," says Cat.

"Well, you don't dance like Bunny," says Mouse. "But I like your way of dancing, too."

The Lost Shoes

The Lost Shoes

The next day, Cat practices dancing whenever she can. The day after that, she would practice dancing, if only she could find the dancing shoes.

Cat is looking for the shoes when there is a knock at the door. When Cat opens the door, she is surprised to see Bunny standing there.

"Hi, Bunny," says Cat. "I'm having a great time with your shoes. You don't need them back yet, do you?"

"Well," says Bunny, "I really do. Can I have them back now? And I'd love to see you dance. Mouse says you're pretty good!"

"Of course," says Cat. She leaves Bunny outside and goes to her room. She looks and looks where she has already looked and looked before. Finally, Cat goes back outside to see Bunny.

"Here, Bunny," she says. "I can't quite find your dancing shoes, but you can have my new sneakers."

"No, Cat," says Bunny, sadly shaking her head. "I need my dancing shoes."

Bunny walks home slowly. When she gets home, Mouse is waiting for her in her room.

"Hi, Bunny! I can see you're upset," says Mouse. "What's wrong?"

"I've just been to Cat's house to get my dancing shoes," says Bunny. "She told me they're lost. I shouldn't have let her borrow them!"

"I've seen Cat's room," says Mouse. "It is very, very messy!" she adds.

"What am I going to do?" asks Bunny. "I wanted to be friendly and helpful. I wanted to trust Cat, but now I need my dancing shoes, and they're lost!"

"I have an idea, Bunny," says Mouse. "I'll help Cat clean her room. Maybe that way I can find the shoes."

"That's a great idea!" says Bunny. "But I can't let you do that by yourself. They're my shoes, after all. We'll both help Cat clean her room."

Bunny starts to feel better. The two friends head back to Cat's house.

The Lost Shoes

The Lost Shoes

When Bunny and Mouse get to Cat's house, they find Cat sitting on the front porch, her head hanging low.

"Hello, Cat," says Mouse with a serious voice. "We've come to help you clean your room so we can find Bunny's dancing shoes."

"But I've already looked everywhere," says Cat. "I'm afraid it's a lost cause."

"Lost shoes, you mean," says Mouse. "Come on, Cat, don't just mope. Let's get to work!"

Bunny and Mouse can tell that Cat feels very badly about the lost shoes.

Bunny, Mouse, and Cat go to Cat's room. They look in and under the heaps and piles of clothes, books, and toys. They look through all the drawers and bins and boxes. Bunny can hardly believe the mess!

Mouse burrows under things and checks under the bed. Bunny runs all over the room tossing things from one pile to another pile. Cat is beginning to think that they will never find the lost shoes in her very messy room.

Finally Mouse looks around and says, "I think I see the problem here. We aren't cleaning! We're just moving the mess around!"

"Let's try to find a good place to put everything neatly away," says Bunny.

"How about clothes in the closet and in drawers," says Mouse happily.

"And books on the bookshelf," says Bunny.

"And toys in the toy box," adds Cat.

At last Cat's room begins to look tidy. There is only a pile of clothes left on the floor to put away.

Bunny is beginning to worry that they will never find her lost shoes.

Cat says, "You two rest while I put away these clothes. I was using them for costumes when I danced." Cat picks up the clothes one by one and puts them away neatly. Finally Cat uncovers Bunny's dancing shoes.

"Bunny! Here are your shoes!" cries Cat happily. She holds out the shoes to Bunny, who jumps for joy.

Mouse starts clapping. "I knew we could find them!" she says.

"Thank you!" says Bunny. "I'm so glad to have my dancing shoes back."

"I didn't mean to lose them," says Cat.

"I know," says Bunny, giving Cat a hug.

"Now that your room is tidy, maybe you'll know where things are," says Mouse.

Cat laughs. "I hope I can keep it this clean! It's so nice to know where things are for a change."

Bunny, Mouse, and Cat go out together into the warm sunshine. They feel so good that they do a happy dance together.

"Let's call this dance Happy Ending," says Cat.

"And I say that Cat is a pretty fine dancer," says Mouse happily.

"I agree," adds Bunny.

"Thank you," says Cat as she twirls around.

Treasure Hunt

Written by Sarah Toast

It is a beautiful blue-sky day, but Puppy is indoors. A big box has arrived at Puppy's house. It is from Puppy's great-granddog.

Puppy is excited as he opens the box. In it are wonderful old books about fun and adventure.

As Puppy looks through the pictures in a fine old book about exploring, something slips out from between the pages and lands at Puppy's feet.

Puppy picks up the old, brittle paper and carefully unfolds it. There, clearly labeled, is a map! A treasure map!

Dear Grandpup,
    I hope you look through the fine old books
I have sent you and find this treasure map. I made
this map when I buried the treasure many years
ago. Have fun on your treasure hunt!

                    Pats and scratches,
                    Great-Granddog

Treasure Hunt

Treasure Hunt

"Wow! A real treasure hunt!" says Puppy.

He packs cheese and crackers and juice in his backpack. He puts the map in a special pocket where it will be very safe. Then Puppy sets out to round up some friends.

Bear is out for a walk. "Hello, Puppy," says Bear. "I'm going to the woods to climb a tree."

"I'm going that way, too. I'm going on a treasure hunt!" says Puppy. "Why don't you come with me?"

It is not long before Bunny leaps into their path. "I call this dance Leaping Toward Blue," says Bunny, as she jumps toward the sky and lands gracefully.

"Come with us!" says Puppy. "We're going to find hidden treasure!"

Bunny is very excited and gracefully leaps into the air again.

"What about me?" says a small voice. Mouse strides into their path. "Just because you have to look down to see me doesn't mean I can't help find hidden treasure!"

"Of course it doesn't," says Puppy. "Come with us!"

"The first thing we have to do is study the map," says Puppy. He takes off his backpack and gets out the map. Puppy, Bear, and Bunny all crowd around to look.

"What about me?" says Mouse. Puppy puts the map on the ground so Mouse can see it, too.

"We're on the right path to the woods," says Puppy. "When we get to the lake, we'll walk halfway around, and then we'll dig for treasure!"

"This is going to be so much fun," Bear says.

The treasure hunters follow the path into the deepening woods. Soon all they can see are tall trees blocking the sky and thick bushes crowding the ground.

"I don't know if we are still heading toward the lake," says Puppy.

"I'll climb a tall tree and see what I can see," says Bear. When he is up very high, Bear calls down, "I see sunlight sparkling on water! The lake is straight ahead!"

The others cheer. They can hardly wait to find the buried treasure.

Bear climbs down from the tree, and the group continues through the woods. They walk and walk. All four friends are getting hot, tired, and hungry.

"We should stop for a rest," says Puppy. They sit down in a shady spot and share the snacks that Puppy and Bear have brought in their backpacks. Then they enjoy the cool breeze that rustles the leaves.

"I wonder how much farther the lake is," says Mouse.

"I'll leap on ahead and see how far we have to go!" says Bunny. In only a few minutes, Bunny returns.

"We're almost there!" she says.

Puppy, Bear, and Mouse join Bunny as they push forward. Mouse can hardly wait to reach the water. Bear is getting tired. Bunny is getting hot. Puppy hopes they do not have far to walk once they cross the lake.

They see more blue sky as the trees thin. Then they walk out of the woods and onto the sandy shore of the big lake.

"Now we know where the cool breeze was coming from!" says Puppy.

Puppy, Bear, Bunny, and Mouse walk right up to the water's edge to cool their toes in the lake. Suddenly Hippo's friendly face rises out of the water.

"Hi!" says Hippo. "Bet you thought I was just a bump on a log!"

"Hi, Hippo!" says Puppy. "We're going to dig up buried treasure on the other side of the lake."

"It sure is a big lake," says Mouse. "It's an awfully long walk around to the other side."

"You don't have to walk around," says Hippo. "I'll take you across on my back!"

"Hooray for Hippo!" the friends cheer.

Puppy is the first to ride across. His feet get wet. Then Hippo comes back for Bunny. Her feet get wet, too.

When Hippo returns for another rider, Bear tells Mouse, "You'll get all wet if you ride by yourself. Jump up on my backpack, and we'll ride across together."

Mouse enjoys her ride, but wishes she was bigger so she could go by herself.

Treasure Hunt

Hippo, Bear, and Mouse join Puppy and Bunny on the far beach.

"Let's look at the map again," says Puppy.

"It shows a big X just this side of a very small tree," says Bear.

Puppy goes to work and digs a big hole a little way from a small tree. There is no treasure hidden there.

"Here's another small tree!" says Bunny. Puppy digs another hole, but finds nothing but rocks and shells.

The friends are very disappointed.

"I need to take a break," says Puppy.

"That map must be as old as the hills," says Hippo. "Maybe someone already dug up the treasure."

"That gives me an idea," says Puppy. "My great-granddog made this map a long time ago. A tree that was small then would be much bigger now."

All of the animals turn and look at the big tree right in front of them. Puppy dashes over and starts digging again.

Puppy digs with all his might for a long time. Finally he uncovers something big.

"I found something," shouts Puppy, "and I don't think it's just a rock!"

Puppy digs some more all around the long shape. At last he uncovers it enough so he can pull it out of the hole. He drops it on the ground in front of his surprised friends.

"What is it?" they all ask. It is something shaped like a tube wrapped up in brown paper and tied tightly with old twine.

When the layers of old stiff paper are peeled away, there is a smaller shape wrapped in checkered cloth and tied with a ribbon.

"I'll untie the ribbon knot," says Bunny. When she has finished, there is a smaller shape wrapped in red and white paper with a label pasted on it.

Bunny can hardly believe her eyes!

Puppy gasps!

Bear and Hippo are amazed!

Mouse tries to get a better view.

Bear reads the label. "Congratulations! You have found the treasure. This little package is full of silver dollars!"

"My stars, can I see it?" asks Hippo. He reaches for the package, but accidentally knocks it out of Bear's paw.

The coins fly toward a big old tree. They land with a thud and roll out of sight.

"Where did they go?" Puppy shouts. They all run up to look. Hippo feels terrible about his clumsiness. He hopes the treasure is not lost forever.

"I see the coins!" says Bunny. "They rolled into the tangle of roots under the tree."

First Puppy, then Bear, then Bunny try to reach the coins, but they are all wedged too far under the tangle of roots.

"They might as well be buried again," says Puppy.

"We'll never get them back now," Bunny says.

"It's hopeless," Bear adds.

Then Mouse says, "Don't I always say small is terrific?"

Mouse dives into the tangle of roots and disappears. The others nervously wait to see if she can find all the coins in the tangled roots.

Then the coins start to move. First one, then another is inched forward. At last Mouse frees all the coins from the roots and rolls them to the waiting group of friends.

"Here's your treasure, Puppy," says Mouse proudly.

The others cheer for Mouse!

"All of you came with me on this adventure," says Puppy. "All of you helped. We'll share the treasure!"

"Let's put the coins in your backpack to carry them home," says Hippo. "I'll take everyone across the lake."

"First we should fill in the holes Puppy dug," says Bunny, "so we leave the shore just like we found it."

It does not take long for the five friends to fill in the three big holes. Then Hippo takes Bear, Bunny, and Puppy back across the lake. This time Mouse rides on Puppy's backpack to safeguard the treasure.

The friends cross the beach and come again to the dense woods.

They are very tired but very happy. They follow the long path back through the woods and then across the meadow toward home.

"That was a lot of fun," Bear says.

"I'm so glad we found the treasure," Bunny adds as she gracefully twirls around.

"Well, if it wasn't for Mouse, we wouldn't have gotten the treasure back," Hippo reminds them. He is still feeling sad that he knocked the treasure into the tree roots in the first place.

"I'm just glad I could help," Mouse says. She does not want Hippo to feel bad. After all, accidents happen.

"Thank you all for helping me find the treasure," says Puppy. "Each of you helped in a special way."

"Aw, shucks," says Hippo. "It was lots of fun."

"Thank you, Puppy, for sharing with us!" say Bear, Bunny, and Mouse.

Learning Something New

Written by Brian Conway

One sunny summer day, Puppy leaves his house early. He is going to the park to meet his friends. He hops on his tricycle and pedals down the street.

Puppy's little trike is getting old. The paint is fading, and it has one wobbly wheel in back. That wobbly wheel makes his tricycle hard to ride. It really slows Puppy down.

Puppy is getting too old for his little trike. When he was smaller, the tricycle was just the right size for him. But Puppy is growing now.

Every time Puppy pedals, his legs keep hitting the handlebars! That really slows Puppy down, too.

Puppy pedals as fast as he can, but he never goes very fast at all. He huffs and puffs, but he is hardly getting anywhere at all!

"I could go faster if I got off and walked!" Puppy grumbles to himself.

Puppy walks the rest of the way to the park. He pulls his old tricycle along behind him.

At last Puppy arrives at the park. His friends are already there, riding their bicycles along the paths.

"What took you so long?" his friends ask.

"I left early," answers Puppy, "but I'm still the last one here!"

Puppy's friends take one look at Puppy's wobbly little tricycle. Then they know what took him so long.

Hippo stops by on his big bike. Hippo was Puppy's first friend to have a two-wheeler.

"I remember when I outgrew my tricycle," Hippo says. "I'd get on, and no matter how hard I pedaled, I couldn't make it go."

"That's what happened to me," says Puppy. "It took me forever to ride two blocks!"

"You should start thinking about getting a new bike," says Hippo. "Everyone else has two-wheelers now."

Pig and Cat zoom by on their speedy bikes. They ring their handlebar bells at Puppy. "See you after the race!" they call to him.

Puppy cannot join a race with his old tricycle, and he cannot play with his friends as long as they ride their bikes all day! Puppy is really feeling left out. He pulls his trike away from the park.

Puppy stops at the bicycle shop on the way home. He sees a lot of super bikes in the window. He sees shiny red bikes, little green bikes, and sleek blue bikes with yellow racing stripes. There are bikes with big, bouncy tires and even bicycles built for two!

"These bikes all cost so much!" Puppy says, his breath fogging up the bicycle shop window. "I don't have enough money to buy one!"

Puppy does not need a fancy racing bike. He just wants a simple two-wheeler. He could even do without a bell on the handlebars.

"Bell or no bell," he sighs, "these bikes still cost way too much!"

Feeling sad, Puppy walks home, pulling his tricycle behind him.

Puppy walks by the bicycle shop every day for a week. He stops to stare in the window. He looks at the price tags, but he could never afford a new bike.

Puppy has been saving his allowance, but he would have to save for a very long time before he had enough money to buy a new bike.

"I'll never get a two-wheeler," Puppy says to himself.

One day, Hippo sees a very sad Puppy staring at a red bike in the window of the bike shop. "Are you going to get a new two-wheeler?" Hippo asks.

"I don't have enough money," Puppy answers. "I hardly have enough for a set of training wheels!"

"Why don't you get those now?" Hippo suggests. "They will remind you to keep saving money until you have enough to buy the rest of the bike!"

"That's a great idea!" says Puppy. "I'll do it!"

Puppy saves his money for weeks and weeks, but he still has not saved enough to buy a new bike.

Puppy is feeling lonely all summer long. Most days, his friends like to ride to the park. When they do, they leave Puppy behind.

Puppy feels a little bit better a few weeks later. It is his favorite time of year. His birthday is just around the corner! His friends always plan a big party for him.

When the big day comes, though, nobody says a word about it! Puppy expects to receive a few little gifts from his friends. Instead, Puppy just gets bad news.

"We're riding to the park," says Hippo. "We'll see you later."

As he walks slowly back home, Puppy says, "This is the worst birthday ever!"

But when he gets to his house, his friends are there to greet him.

"Surprise!" they shout. And they wheel out his birthday gift.

"A new bike!" Puppy says. "You guys are the best!"

"This is the greatest birthday ever!" Puppy says. "But how did you have enough money to buy me a new bike?"

"It's not really new," says Hippo. "It used to belong to Bear's older brother."

"He got too big for it," Bear explains. "But we fixed it up for you so it's as good as new!"

"It's new to me!" Puppy exclaims. "I can't wait to ride it!"

Hippo helps Puppy put his training wheels on the new two-wheeler. Then they are off for Puppy's first ride with his friends in a long time.

"We'll race you to the park!" says Pig, zooming ahead.

Puppy pedals as fast as he can, but he is still getting used to the big new bike. Puppy is the last one to arrive at the park.

"What took you so long?" laughs Pig. "Are those baby wheels slowing you down?"

Puppy feels sad. He parks his birthday gift in the bike rack and watches his friends zoom by him.

Hippo stops to see what is wrong.

"Do you have a flat tire, or what?" asks Hippo. "Come ride with us!"

"I can't keep up with you," Puppy sighs. "Not with these training wheels."

Hippo offers to pedal more slowly, and Cat says she will, too. But Puppy does not want them to slow down for him. Pig would only make fun of them.

"I am a year older now," Puppy says. "I want to ride as fast as everyone else!"

Puppy knows it is not that easy. It takes practice to learn to ride a two-wheeler.

"One ride with training wheels is not enough," says Hippo. "You have to get used to a taller bike."

Hippo uses his own bike to show Puppy a few important things about riding a two-wheeler. He shows him the best ways to keep the bike from tipping over.

"You can put your leg down if you feel like you're falling," Hippo says.

Puppy does not want to fall over. He practices for a while with the training wheels.

The next day, Puppy rides his new bike to the park. With training wheels, the bike is easy to ride. Puppy's new bike goes a lot faster than his old tricycle did. But Puppy is still the last one to get to the park.

Hippo is waiting for him at the bike rack.

"I remembered how I learned to ride without training wheels," Hippo says. "The best way to learn is to try it! And if you're ready, I'll show you how."

Puppy is still a little bit scared that he will fall over. But he really wants to go faster.

"I'm ready!" says Puppy.

Together, Puppy and Hippo take off the training wheels. Puppy feels shaky when he climbs on the seat. He feels like he is tipping over, but Hippo helps to hold the bike up.

"You take care of the pedaling and steering," says Hippo, "and I'll hold the bike up straight."

While Puppy pedals slowly, Hippo runs alongside him.

Puppy is glad to have a friend like Hippo. Hippo helps to keep Puppy safe, and he never teases Puppy for being afraid of falling.

Together, they ride around the park a few times. Puppy is learning quickly. He already knows how to pedal and turn. He has a good feeling for keeping his balance.

Hippo is starting to get tired. On their next turn around the park, Hippo puffs, "This will have to be our last lap of the day, so go as fast as you can!"

Puppy pumps the pedals as fast as he can. He likes to feel the wind on his fur!

"Am I going too fast for you, Hippo?" Puppy asks.

Hippo does not answer. He is not holding onto the bike anymore! Hippo let go when Puppy started pedaling quickly. Puppy has been riding a two-wheeler all by himself!

"I knew you could do it!" Hippo calls.

Learning Something New

By now all of Puppy's friends have come to see him ride. Puppy finds Hippo in the crowd. He is waving at Puppy.

"Now come back!" Hippo calls. "Just keep pedaling until you get here!" Puppy rides toward his friends. Even Pig cheers him on.

Puppy keeps the bike up the whole ride back. He also remembers to use his leg when he stops, just like Hippo taught him to do.

"Congratulations on your first solo ride!" says Hippo.

"I've never ridden so fast before!" Puppy says. "But I didn't do it myself. You helped me learn how!"

Pig picks up Puppy's training wheels. "I guess you won't be needing these anymore," he says.

"Later, I'll put them in the garage with my old tricycle," Puppy says. "Right now, though, I have a race to ride!"

While Pig and the others scurry to their bikes, Puppy pedals ahead of the pack.

Litterbug Bear

Written by Brian Conway

At lunchtime Bear eats slower than his friends do. While his friends hurry so they will have more time to play, Bear takes his time.

"I'll join you in a minute," says Bear, as his friends run to the playground.

The best part of lunch for Bear is his dessert. Bear always eats a chocolate candy bar. On his walk out to the playground, he peels off the wrapper and eats the candy bar in just two big bites! It is really the only thing Bear does quickly.

Today Mouse and Turtle are late finishing their lunches. They follow Bear out to the playground.

"I've never seen anyone eat a candy bar so fast!" Mouse whispers to Turtle.

Turtle cannot believe it either. "Did he eat the wrapper, too?" he asks.

Turtle's question is answered when he looks down at Mouse. Her foot is stuck on Bear's sticky wrapper!

"Bear dropped the wrapper on the ground!" Mouse complains to the others. "He never looked back!"

"I don't think Bear would litter on purpose," says Puppy. "Maybe he was in a hurry."

Cat cannot believe it. "I have never seen Bear hurry anywhere!" she says. "But I've never seen him litter either."

"I'm sure if we talk to him," Puppy adds, "we'll find out it's all a big mistake."

Mouse finds Bear first. She shows him how the wrapper made her clean yellow dress all spotted and sticky.

"Why would you litter when the trash can is only a few steps away?" Puppy asks Bear.

"Who littered?" asks Bear, still licking the chocolate from his furry fingers.

"Well," says Mouse, "sloppy candy bar wrappers don't just fall from the sky!"

Bear looks around the playground. He does not see a candy bar wrapper around. The wind has blown it away.

"What wrapper?" he asks.

The next day, Puppy, Mouse, and Bunny finish their lunch first. They hide behind a tree and wait for Bear.

Bear is the last one to finish his lunch. As he walks away from the lunch table, Bear opens his candy bar. After two quick bites, his candy bar is gone, and the wrapper is on the ground behind him!

Puppy and Bunny cannot believe what they saw. They run up to stop Bear.

Mouse gets there first. "We caught you in the act!" she shouts at Bear.

Bear looks puzzled, so Bunny picks up the sticky wrapper. "Do you have any idea where this came from?" she asks.

"Oh, that," says Bear carelessly. "That used to be on my candy bar."

"You littered, Bear, and that's not right," says Puppy.

Bear just shrugs and walks away. "It's only one little wrapper," he calls. "What's all the fuss about?"

Litterbug Bear

Nobody wants to play with Bear that day. He sits alone in the sandbox, slowly piling up sand for a special castle he is making.

Puppy gets the others together. "Bear won't listen to us," says Puppy. "He doesn't seem to care about the mess he's making."

"We have to show Bear how terrible it is when he litters!" says Bunny.

Bunny wants to take Bear's candy bars away from him. Mouse wants to rub chocolate on Bear's fur! But Puppy and Skunk have a plan that will solve their problem. It will teach Bear a lesson about littering, too.

"We'll pick up after Bear for a week," Puppy says. "We'll save every wrapper he tosses on the ground."

"At the end of the week," says Skunk, "we'll have a mess that's so big even Bear will notice it!"

All week long, they keep an eye on Bear. Whenever he drops a wrapper, they pick up the sticky mess and put it in Puppy's backpack.

In Ms. Hen's class the next week, it is Bunny and Mouse's turn to give a book report. The book they picked is all about littering. Bunny and Mouse tell the class what they have learned.

"Trash piles up in streets, in parks, in rivers and lakes, and even in playgrounds!" says Mouse.

Everyone looks at Bear. He is listening, but he does not look a bit sorry.

Bunny tells the class, "Littering can make a beautiful place look ugly."

"It can make a playground look like a garbage dump!" Mouse adds.

At last Bear speaks up. "What about one little wrapper?" he asks. "How can that make a difference?"

Tearing a small piece from his pad of paper, Bear holds it in his hand for a moment. Then he lets it drop to the floor. "The wind takes it away," he says, "and nobody ever sees it again."

Bunny and Mouse are shocked! They worked hard on their book report, but Bear does not seem to care.

Mouse has a question for Bear. "When the wind takes a piece of trash away, where do you think it goes?" she asks. Bear just shrugs.

"It ends up in somebody's yard, in the street, in the woods, or in a stream," Bunny says.

Bear looks around the room. His classmates look at him, then they look at the piece of paper on the floor. Bear does not budge.

Ms. Hen agrees with Bunny. "If everyone dropped just one little piece of paper in my classroom," she says, "it would pile up into a huge mess!"

Ms. Hen holds the wastebasket in front of Bear. She reminds him that whenever anybody drops something in her classroom, they have to pick it up.

Bear slowly picks up the paper he dropped and puts it in the wastebasket.

Bunny wants to know if Bear has been listening to their book report.

"What did you learn about littering, Bear?" she asks.

"I learned to keep Ms. Hen's classroom clean," he answers. "But there's no rule saying we cannot litter on the playground."

Mouse is still upset because Bear just does not understand. She opens a book with pictures.

First she shows Bear a picture of a trash can. "This is a trash can. This is the only place we should put our trash," she says.

Then Mouse points to pictures of trash — papers, cans, and plastic bags. The trash is stuck in fences. It is littered in piles around trees in the forest.

"This is not a trash can," Mouse points out. "It's that easy to make a difference."

Bear looks through the book. He sees a bottle, an old can, a candy wrapper, and a tire in a river. Bear starts to feel sick.

Litterbug Bear

After Bunny and Mouse's book report, Bear eats his lunch more slowly than usual.

The others finish their lunches quickly. They rush out to the playground. It is time to finish their plan, and put an end to Bear's littering, once and for all.

Puppy empties his backpack. Over the past week, Bear's friends have collected a big pile of sticky, crusty candy bar wrappers!

"Where should we leave the pile?" Puppy asks.

"It has to be where Bear will see it!" Skunk adds.

Mouse knows just the place. She carries a handful of wrappers over to the sandbox. The others grab a few wrappers and follow her.

"This looks like a good place for a trash can!" Mouse laughs. Everyone agrees that the sand castle will look perfect if it has a flag made out of a candy bar wrapper on top. Mouse adds the finishing touch.

The friends wait for Bear to finish his lunch.

Bear is feeling much better by dessert time. As he walks out to the playground, he finishes his candy bar as quickly as ever! Then Bear lets the candy bar wrapper fall to the ground, just like he always does.

"Same old litterbug Bear," whispers Mouse. "Well, we'll see about that."

Bear's friends follow him over to the sandbox.

"Hey!" Bear shouts when he sees the pile of wrappers all over his sand castle. "Who made this mess?"

"It's your mess, Bear," says Puppy. "We put it there, but it's your mess."

Bear sees that the wrappers are from his favorite kind of candy bar. Mouse tells Bear how they picked up after him for a whole week.

"That's only one week of your littering, Bear," she says. "If we kept it up, we could fill the whole sandbox!"

Bear was very proud of his sand castle, but he does not like the way it looks now.

Litterbug Bear

"I can see now how littering can ruin something beautiful," Bear admits.

"We have to be proud of our playground and our town," Puppy explains, "and work to keep it beautiful. It's not very hard to make a difference."

Bear understands. He carefully picks up the wrappers in the sandbox. He carries the pile to the nearest trash can.

"That was easy!" Bear says. "I promise I won't litter again. All these wrappers are ugly!"

While his friends cheer, Bear suddenly runs back toward the schoolhouse.

"Where is he going?" asks Mouse.

"I've never seen him run so fast!" says Turtle.

Bear hurries to the spot where he dropped his candy bar after lunch today. The wind has not carried it away yet. Bear picks up the wrapper and puts it in the trash can.

"If you're going to make a difference," he calls back to his friends, "why not start today?"

Good Manners

Written by Dana Richter

It is the start of a new school day for Ms. Hen and her students. "Good morning, class," Ms. Hen says. "Aren't we all full of talk and laughter today!"

Ms. Hen's students are too busy talking. They do not even hear her. Ms. Hen begins the day by reading a book to her class. Puppy and his friends can barely sit still through the whole story.

After the story, Ms. Hen turns to the chalkboard and begins the day's lesson. "Let's begin with math. We're going to learn all about addition," explains Ms. Hen.

She shows her class an example on the board, but no one pays attention.

"When are we going to have show-and-tell?" blurts out Puppy. "I want to tell the whole class all about my fun adventures!"

"And I could show you my new dance!" adds Bunny.

"I'd rather go on a field trip," says Cat.

"Oh, yes!" agrees Pig. "We could go to the circus and be clowns for a day." Pig makes everyone laugh.

"When is recess?" shouts Mouse.

Good Manners

As Ms. Hen turns from the blackboard, Turtle asks, "Ms. Hen, how do you do addition?"

"Asking questions when it is not your turn to talk is not nice at all," says Ms. Hen.

The class grows silent. They all look down at their desks. They know Ms. Hen is unhappy with them.

"Does anyone know what rude means?" asks Ms. Hen.

"I do! I do!" shouts Pig. "It's when you don't use good manners."

Cat says using good manners means sharing the swings at recess. Puppy agrees and adds that if you have good manners, you listen to your friends when they talk.

"Yes," agrees Ms. Hen. "And good manners are when you wait to be called on before you speak in class. Having good manners means saying 'please' and 'thank you' to your friends. Good manners are when you treat others how you would like to be treated."

Puppy wishes he had used good manners this morning. He interrupted Cat and Bunny on the way to school today. He really wanted to tell them about a new game he had just learned to play.

The class gets very quiet. Ms. Hen thinks her students have learned their lesson about using good manners.

Ms. Hen asks all of her students to go to the science center. Today they will be conducting a new experiment. She tells them that they will all have to listen very carefully to her instructions.

Then Ms. Hen shows them how to make flowers change colors. Everyone is very excited about making their white flowers turn red, blue, and green. But they forget about using good manners.

"I'm going to make my flower red," says Mouse. "Red is the prettiest!"

"I think a nice blue flower would be the most fun!" says Hippo.

"Try and catch this!" says Skunk to Puppy. Skunk flies a paper airplane across the room. Puppy jumps up and catches it.

Ms. Hen peeks up from her experiment. "This doesn't look like good manners to me," says Ms. Hen.

Then she gets an idea for a new experiment, one that will teach her students a lesson about good manners.

"I have an idea," says Ms. Hen. "All of you are going to conduct an experiment for me. For the rest of the school day, I want you all to forget about using any good manners."

Puppy and his friends can hardly believe what they are hearing!

"This is going to be the best experiment we ever did!" exclaims Cat.

"There will be no saying 'please' and 'thank you' for me," adds Puppy.

"And I won't share or take turns if I don't want to," says Turtle.

"We all can talk and ask Ms. Hen questions whenever we want," says Hippo.

"And we don't have to be nice if we don't want to!" says Mouse uncertainly. Mouse does not think she likes the sound of the experiment at all. She worries that all of her friends will be mean to each other.

Ms. Hen knows bad manners makes teaching very hard. But she thinks the lesson her students will learn about good manners is more important.

The bell rings for recess. Ms. Hen's students jump up and rush through the door.

Usually, Ms. Hen's students are not allowed to push and run to the door. But in the spirit of her good manners experiment, Ms. Hen just quietly watches them push and shove each other.

"Look out!" calls Hippo as he pushes past his classmates. "I may be slow, but I sure am big!"

"Hey, that's not fair," yells Pig.

"Hippo, wait your turn!" adds Cat.

Pig and Cat want to be the first ones on the playground, but Hippo squeezes out the door instead. The rest of the class stampedes to the door after them.

"Last one to the playground is a rotten egg!" hollers Skunk, as he runs past Mouse and spins her around.

"Hey, wait for me!" Mouse calls after her friends. No one hears her little voice but Ms. Hen.

Mouse looks at Ms. Hen, hoping she will say something about her rude classmates. But Ms. Hen keeps her eyes on the papers she is grading.

Good Manners

Skunk and Turtle are the first ones to the swings. Bear and Bunny want to swing, too. They wait for their turn, but Skunk and Turtle just keep swinging.

"You've been swinging for a long time," says Bear. "May Bunny and I have a turn?"

"No, I don't think so," says Skunk.

"We don't feel like sharing today," chimes in Turtle.

"Swinging is our favorite thing to do at recess," pleads Bunny. But Skunk and Turtle do not want to share today. They just ignore Bear and Bunny.

At the same time, Puppy tries to organize a game with Hippo, Cat, Pig, and Mouse.

"I want to show you all a new game," says Puppy.

"I think we should play kickball," says Hippo.

"But I want to play dodgeball," whines Cat.

"Why don't we play baseball?" shouts Mouse, as she jumps up and down trying to get some attention.

"I don't want to play any of those games," snorts Pig. "I want to play hide-and-seek."

The friends spend so much time bickering, recess is over before they can choose a game at all.

Back in the classroom, the students settle in for reading hour. It is Hippo's turn to read today. He is really excited to share his favorite story with all of his friends. He begins to read about a king and his castle.

His friends do not pay much attention to Hippo. Instead they talk to each other.

"If I were a king I would have a castle made of candy and go on great adventures," says Puppy.

"I would be your court jester and make you laugh all the time," chuckles Pig.

"I wouldn't want to be a king. I would be a beautiful princess," says Cat. "I would wear beautiful dresses all the time," she adds.

"And I would be the queen!" adds Mouse.

Ms. Hen watches from her desk. She feels sorry for Hippo. She knows that Hippo really wanted to share his favorite story with his friends.

Now they are not even listening to him. If they were using their good manners, they would be quiet and pay attention to Hippo and his story.

Good Manners

"Now that reading hour is over, let's move on to English," says Ms. Hen. "This might be confusing, so pay attention and concentrate on your work." She turns to the chalkboard and writes a long sentence.

"I don't understand this at all," says Turtle. "Do you know how to do it, Bunny?"

"No, but if I did I wouldn't share it with you, like you wouldn't share the swings with me and Bear at recess!" Bunny replies.

"Ms. Hen, do you put a question mark at the end of a sentence?" Puppy cries out from his desk.

"Where did that comma come from?" asks Bear, completely confused.

"Maybe if you all were quiet and listened you would find out," Cat says loudly.

When Ms. Hen turns around, the class is in quite a state. Everyone is shouting questions at the same time and squirming in their seats.

"Any questions?" Ms. Hen asks with a satisfied tone in her voice.

"Now that the day is nearly over," says Ms Hen, "I'm curious to know what you thought of my experiment."

Mouse is the first one to raise her hand. Ms. Hen nods to her and Mouse speaks. "I didn't think it was very nice when my friends left me behind at recess."

Bunny raises her hand, too. She waits until Ms. Hen calls on her to speak. "Bear and I didn't get to swing on the swings at recess because Skunk and Turtle didn't want to share with us."

"And recess wasn't any fun when the rest of us couldn't agree on a game to play," adds Puppy, when Ms. Hen calls on him.

Then Hippo raises his hand. "My friends made me feel bad when they didn't listen to me read my story," says Hippo. "Now I know how you feel when we talk and you are trying to teach," he adds.

"So what did these experiences teach you about good manners?" Ms. Hen asks her class. Every student raises a hand.

"I learned that when you use good manners you think of others before yourself," says Mouse.

"I learned that without good manners there would be no sharing, and I like it better when my friends share," says Bunny.

"I learned that it's much more fun to play when you use good manners," adds Puppy.

"And I learned that it's much nicer when the class pays attention when someone else is talking," says Hippo.

Finally, Ms. Hen adds, "Don't you all agree that learning is much harder when the class is loud and you are all asking questions at the same time?"

"Oh, yes!" they all say, nodding their heads excitedly.

"Especially English," says Skunk.

When the school bell rings, the class waits to be dismissed and leaves in a nice, straight line. Puppy even waits and lets Mouse go in front of him. "After you," he says to Mouse.

"No, after you," Mouse says to Puppy.

They both walk out the door together.

"I don't think good manners will be a problem in my class again," Ms. Hen says to herself, smiling.

The Broken Flowerpot

Written by Brian Conway

Recess on the playground is the best time of day for Puppy and his friends. Today they are playing kickball. The game is very close, but Puppy's team is not worried. It is Hippo's turn to kick.

Hippo is the best kickball player in the whole school. Because they have Hippo on their side, Puppy's team always wins!

"We need a good kick, Hippo," Puppy calls. "I know you can do it!"

With one swing of his strong leg, Hippo sends the ball flying! It bounces back to the fence while Hippo runs around the bases.

Hippo may be the best kicker in the school, but he is not the fastest runner. It will be a very close call at home base. Hippo dives to the base.

When the dust clears, Puppy's team starts to cheer. Hippo won the game! Puppy and his friends are the champions for the day!

The Broken Flowerpot

The friends charge back to the classroom. They are still cheering about Hippo's great slide. Hippo is the hero for the day!

Skunk missed the game. Puppy tells him all about it.

"We needed Hippo to score," Puppy says. "Of course, he scored!"

"It was much better than that," Hippo tells them. "I slid on my belly to win the game!"

"It sounds like a fantastic finish!" says Skunk. "I wish I'd seen it!"

Hippo runs to the front of the classroom. "Here," he says, "I'll show you." He takes three ground-shaking steps and dives to the floor.

But here inside Ms. Hen's classroom, Hippo does not have much space for his big slide. He bumps into Ms. Hen's desk by accident.

Before Hippo can stop it, Ms. Hen's favorite flowerpot topples from her desk to the floor. It shatters into a hundred broken pieces.

As soon as she steps into her classroom, Ms. Hen sees the broken flowerpot. Her students watch her.

She looks down at the flowerpot, then she looks up at them. They are all very quiet.

"Oh, dear!" Ms. Hen sighs. "My favorite flowerpot! How could this have happened?"

Everybody in the class shrugs and looks at one another. Puppy and Cat look at Hippo. They think he should stand up and tell the truth about what happened.

While Ms. Hen cleans up, Hippo slowly slides down in his desk. He feels very badly about the accident.

"Nobody knows?" asks Ms. Hen. "I know my flower was on the desk when we all left for recess."

At last Hippo speaks up. "We were all so excited about winning our big kickball game at recess today," says Hippo, "I guess nobody noticed the mess."

"A mess like this is very hard to miss," says Ms. Hen. "But I do know how you all get very excited about your games at recess."

The Broken Flowerpot

The Broken Flowerpot

The students are very quiet while Ms. Hen teaches the class. Nobody says a word until lunchtime.

At the lunch table, everyone has something to say to Hippo. He still feels miserable.

"You already lied once," says Puppy. "You should tell Ms. Hen the truth."

"She will understand," adds Cat. "It was an accident, after all."

Mouse reminds Hippo that a lie only makes things worse. "At first it was just an accident," she tells him. "Now it is an accident with a lie on top of it."

Hippo does not know what to do. He is afraid Ms. Hen will yell at him.

Pig has a different idea. "I would make something up," he says. "Tell Ms. Hen a story about how her flowerpot broke while everybody was away at recess."

"But that's adding a new lie on top of an old lie!" Mouse says sadly.

"But this way, no one gets into trouble!" Pig says.

Hippo returns to the classroom before lunch is over. He still does not know what he will say to Ms. Hen. He wants to tell the truth, but he does not want to get into trouble.

"Um, Ms. Hen," Hippo stutters.

"Yes, Hippo," says Ms. Hen. "Come in. Do you have something to tell me?"

Hippo opens his mouth to tell the truth, but another lie comes out instead. He tells Ms. Hen the students all saw a little airplane flying in dips and loops over the playground during recess today.

"So I was thinking," Hippo says, "maybe the airplane looped in through the window. It could have knocked over your flowerpot!"

"That could be," Ms. Hen says. "Thank you, Hippo."

Relieved, Hippo goes to sit down at his desk. After a moment, Ms. Hen points to her flower.

"My flower needs a bigger pot to grow," she says to Hippo. "Why don't you stay after school to help me plant it again?"

The Broken Flowerpot

The Broken Flowerpot

All afternoon, Hippo is too worried to think about school. He thinks Ms. Hen may want to scold him after school is over.

While his friends play after school, Hippo rushes to the sandbox for his pail and shovel.

Beside the schoolhouse, Hippo busily digs fresh soil for his teacher's flower.

Ms. Hen comes to meet Hippo in the schoolyard. "Thank you for the fresh soil," she says. "This bucket will make a wonderful flowerpot. It won't break like the last one."

Again, Hippo starts to tell Ms. Hen the truth, but another lie comes out instead. He tells her he saw a giant on the playground today.

"This giant stomped across the playground," Hippo lies. "He shook the ground with every step. Maybe all that shaking knocked over your flowerpot."

"That could be," Ms. Hen says. "But I would have noticed a giant on the playground, don't you think? Something else must have knocked over my flowerpot."

Hippo sits next to Puppy on the bus. He tells Puppy what happened after school.

"A giant!" Puppy says. "That is the biggest lie yet!"

Hippo says, "I wanted to tell her the truth, but I was afraid she would be angry. These silly stories kept coming out instead. Now it is much too late."

Puppy knows Ms. Hen is a very understanding teacher. "It is never too late to tell the truth," Puppy tells his worried friend.

Hippo knows Puppy is right. Still, Hippo does not know what he will do.

At home, Hippo is too worried to eat. He has forgotten all about the big game at recess today. He does not think he is a hero anymore. He thinks he is a liar.

Hippo gets into bed. He is so worried, he cannot sleep. He never had trouble sleeping before, and eating was never a problem for Hippo!

Late that night, Hippo decides how he can make everything better.

The next morning, Hippo gets to school before any of his classmates.

He goes straight to Ms. Hen's desk and says, "Ms. Hen, I have something to tell you. It was an accident. I didn't mean it. Then I lied!"

"Slow down, Hippo," says Ms. Hen calmly. "I'm listening to you."

With tears in his eyes, Hippo says he is sorry for breaking her flowerpot. But he is even more sorry for the lies he told.

"I feel terrible," he cries. "I didn't want to lie, but I didn't want to get into trouble, either. Now I know that telling the truth is the most important thing."

Ms. Hen is very glad that Hippo decided to tell the truth. She tells him not to worry about getting into trouble. "You learned your lesson," she says. "You told the truth."

Hippo offers to buy his teacher a new flowerpot, but Ms. Hen is happy with the one she has now, and her flower seems to be, too.

Puppy arrives in class first. He did not see Hippo on the bus, but Puppy hoped to find his friend at school.

Hippo is happy again. He smiles and winks at Puppy as Ms. Hen gets class started.

"I have an announcement to make," says Ms. Hen. "I know who broke my flowerpot."

"Oooo," the class groans. They all look at Hippo.

"I know it was an accident, so no one will be punished," she adds. "Accidents happen, and things get broken, but lies can break something much more important than a flowerpot. Does anybody know what lies can break?"

Hippo says, "Lies can break trust."

"That's right, Hippo," Ms. Hen says proudly. "Trust is something that is very important. With trust in one piece, friendships can grow."

Then Ms. Hen shows the class her new flowerpot, the sturdy bucket from Hippo.

"My flower has a new place to grow," she says. "Even a zooming airplane or a stomping giant will never break it!"

Helping Hands

Written by Brian Conway

Puppy's leg is in a cast. His broken leg still hurts a little. But Puppy's feelings hurt the most. Until his leg is better, Puppy thinks he cannot play with his friends.

Puppy cannot run or jump. He cannot swing on the swings or play in the sand. Puppy cannot ride his bike or play ball with his friends. He cannot do any of the things he and his friends like to do together.

Puppy does not want his friends to treat him differently. He does not want them to know he is hurt.

"I can't do anything," Puppy sighs. "What will my friends say when they see me like this?"

The doctor said Puppy can walk, but only if he uses a clunky pair of crutches. They make Puppy's walk very stiff and slow.

Puppy does not feel like walking. He does not want to go to school today. He does not even think he can walk to the bus stop. He does not want to go anywhere at all.

Puppy does not move from his chair all day. He is surprised when the doorbell rings.

"Who could that be?" Puppy grunts, scrambling for his crutches.

Puppy fumbles with the crutches as he goes to the door. One crutch falls to the ground with a big crash.

"Puppy?" says a voice. "Are you in there?"

"Just a minute," Puppy calls through the door. He sets the crutches aside and opens the door — just a crack. Bear and Cat have come to visit him.

"Where were you today?" asks Cat. "We really missed you at school."

Puppy hides his cast behind the door.

"I had the sniffles," he says, "but I'm better now."

"Great!" says Bear. "So let's go for a bike ride!"

Puppy sighs, "I can't. I have to clean my room."

Bear and Cat can tell something is wrong, but they can ride without Puppy today. "Okay," says Cat. "Well, we'll see you at school tomorrow."

Little Life Lessons

Puppy knows he cannot miss school forever. Sooner or later, his friends will have to find out about his leg. Puppy is worried that his friends will not want to play with him.

With his big cast and clunky crutches, everything takes longer for Puppy. It takes him longer to get ready for school the next morning, and it will take him much longer to get to the bus stop.

Puppy picks up his books and his lunch box. His hands are already full. Now how will Puppy hold his crutches?

"It's my leg that's broken," he sighs. "I never thought I'd need two more hands!"

Puppy is sure he can do it by himself, but walking was never so hard.

Puppy is glad he left home early. He does not want his friends to see him having so much trouble!

Puppy thinks about all the times he ran to the bus stop. He wishes he could run now.

"I won't be able to play tag or kickball at recess," Puppy sobs.

Pig and the others meet Puppy at the bus stop.

"Oh, Puppy, look at you," says Pig. "What happened?"

"No big deal," says Puppy gruffly. "I broke my leg."

Cat looks worried. "Are you okay?" she asks kindly.

"I'm fine, really," Puppy grunts. "I'm the same old Puppy, only with a cast on one leg."

Skunk offers to hold Puppy's books for him, and Pig offers to help Puppy climb aboard the bus.

"No, thanks," Puppy says. "I can do it myself."

Puppy's big cast and clunky crutches make it hard for him to climb the steps. His friends can see that Puppy does not want them to make a fuss over him.

On the bus, Mouse talks about something else. "We have a big game to play at recess today," she says.

Puppy frowns. He cannot play kickball today.

"We'll do our best and win it for Puppy!" says Mouse cheerily. Pig agrees with Mouse and smiles at Puppy.

But that does not cheer up Puppy at all.

Puppy makes it to his desk without any help. But he is already so tired, and the school day has just begun!

"Okay, class, everybody up!" says Ms. Hen. "It's time for our spelling assignment."

Puppy's friends rush to the blackboard. Puppy is still reaching for his crutches.

"Oh, Puppy, you're hurt," says Ms. Hen. "I'm sorry. You can write at your desk."

Puppy does not want to write at his desk. He wants to write on the blackboard, like the rest of his friends.

"No, I'm fine," says Puppy. "I can do it."

Ms. Hen looks worried. Still, Puppy picks himself up from his desk and slowly walks up the aisle. One of his crutches hits a desk, and Puppy starts to tip over!

Turtle and Bunny rush over to hold Puppy up. Puppy is very embarrassed. He will not let them lead him back to his desk.

"I'm fine," he grunts. "I can do it all by myself."

Helping Hands

At recess, Puppy's friends stop to ask him if he needs any help.

"You go on ahead," says Puppy. "I can do it. I'll meet you on the playground."

His friends run out to play. Ms. Hen is still worried about Puppy.

"Your friends want to help you," she says. "Why won't you let them?"

"I don't need their help," Puppy answers. "I'm fine."

"But your leg is in a cast," says Ms. Hen, "and you don't seem fine. You are not acting like the Puppy I know. You did not even thank your friends for keeping you from falling!"

Puppy sighs, "I can't run or play. I can hardly walk!"

"Your friends understand," says Ms. Hen.

"Sure, they want to help me," says Puppy. "But they won't want to play with me anymore."

"Don't worry, Puppy," says Ms. Hen. "Your friends will find a way to include you in their fun."

On his clunky crutches, Puppy carries himself toward the playground. Puppy cannot play kickball, but he can still watch his friends play. From the playground, though, Puppy can see that none of his friends are playing kickball!

"Puppy!" his friends call from a picnic table. "We're over here!"

Mouse runs over to meet Puppy.

"We can't play kickball without our best player!" she says. "Our games can wait until you're better."

Puppy's friends have set up a different kind of game. It's a board game that Puppy can play, too!

"Soon your leg will be as good as new," says Bunny.

"We don't mind waiting for you," says Bear. "You're our best friend."

"So let's have fun while we're waiting!" Skunk says.

Puppy is overjoyed! "You mean, you still think I'm fun to be around?" he asks.

"Of course," says Cat. "You're the same old Puppy, only with a cast on one leg!"

Helping Hands

"I was really worried you wouldn't want to play with me anymore," Puppy tells his friends on the way back to class.

"Don't be silly, Puppy," says Turtle.

Puppy smiles and thanks his friends. They promise to help him get better.

"You helped me when my bike had a flat tire," Pig reminds him.

"And you brought me my homework when I was sick," says Skunk.

Puppy lets his friends help him up the steps. He cannot wait to tell Ms. Hen how his friends helped him.

Ms. Hen has planned an art project for the class.

"Everybody get some finger paint," she says. Smiling at Puppy, she adds, "Everybody but Puppy, that is. We're all going to sign Puppy's cast!"

Each of Puppy's friends presses a painted hand into Puppy's white cast. Soon Puppy's cast is covered with colorful handprints.

"These are all your helping hands!" says Ms. Hen.

The day finally comes when Puppy's leg is better. Without a cast and crutches, everything is easier for Puppy. He runs to the bus stop to meet his friends, just like he used to.

His friends are there, clapping for him. Puppy happily hops up every step to get on the bus.

"Ta-da!" he says. His friends clap again.

In class, Ms. Hen calls everybody up to the blackboard. Puppy is the first one there. His friends all giggle and clap for him again.

"It looks like your friends are clapping their helping hands for you!" says Ms. Hen.

Puppy is the star for the day. His friends give him a big card they made with Ms. Hen after school. It says in big letters, "Welcome Back!" It is decorated with all the colorful handprints that had been on his cast.

"Thanks to all my helping hands," Puppy says, "I'm back and better than ever!"

Puppy is very happy he can walk, run, and play again.

But Puppy is even happier to have such wonderful friends who will help him when he needs it.

It does not take long for Puppy to be able to run and jump as well as he could before he broke his leg.

He can swing on the swings and play in the sand. Puppy can ride a bike and play ball with his friends. He can do all the things he and his friends like to do.

At recess Puppy's team has a big game to play today.

"You're up, Puppy," says Mouse. "Kick us a whopper!" Puppy has been waiting for this day for a long time.

Puppy's leg is stronger than ever! He kicks a home run on his first try! Puppy runs around the bases while his friends clap their helping hands.

"I'm so glad I'm better," Puppy tells his friends after the game. "Now I can do everything my friends like to do! I can even help anyone who needs it!"

"Well, you sure helped us win today!" says Mouse. "That's a great start!"

Friends Share

Written by Brian Conway

Bear and Hippo are having fun on the playground together. They take turns on the slide. "After you," says Hippo kindly.

They take turns on the swing. "I think it's your turn to go first," Bear says politely.

They share a ride on the teeter-totter. Bear goes up, and Hippo goes down. Hippo goes up, and Bear goes down. Bear and Hippo make a good team.

At the monkey bars, the friends cannot remember whose turn it is to go first.

"You should go first," says Hippo.

"No, I think you should go first," says Bear.

While they are talking it over, Hippo and Bear look down at the ground. They see the edge of a little green piece of paper poking out from the sand.

Together, they stoop down to pick it up. Hippo reaches for it, and Bear reaches for it. They grab it at exactly the same time. The little paper is a crisp, green dollar bill!

Friends Share

Bear and Hippo's eyes light up!

"Wow!" they shout at exactly the same time. "A dollar!" They take a look around the playground. Bear looks to the left, and Hippo looks to the right. The park is not very crowded. Nobody seems to be looking for anything.

But the two friends cannot celebrate yet. The money is not theirs. Neither of them has lost a dollar. Somebody else must have lost it.

"Someone might really need that money," Bear worries, "to buy food."

"Or somebody might need it to take the bus home tonight," adds Hippo.

Bear wonders, "What if it was somebody's lucky dollar bill and they lost it?"

"If they lost it," Hippo jokes, "it isn't very lucky, is it?"

"And it's our lucky dollar now," Bear chuckles.

Still, Hippo and Bear decide to wait and see if anyone comes looking for the dollar. They just cannot agree on who gets to hold their lucky discovery!

Bear and Hippo wait at the monkey bars for a long time. Nobody comes looking for the dollar.

"Well, we've waited," says Bear. "Can we keep it now?"

"Not yet," says Hippo. "I think we should ask around."

Hippo and Bear set off together through the park. First they meet Skunk. He is cutting across the playground on his way back from the library.

"Hey, Skunk!" Bear calls to him. "Have you lost anything today?"

"I almost forgot my library card," Skunk says, "but I don't think I've lost anything."

"We found a dollar on the playground," Hippo explains. "It's not yours, is it?"

Hippo hopes the dollar does not belong to Skunk.

"I have not been on the playground all day," says Skunk. "And besides, I don't have any money to lose!"

Hippo and Bear ask Skunk what they should do next.

"If I had a dollar," Skunk answers, "I would buy a new book with it."

Friends Share

Hippo and Bear walk to the other end of the playground where they see their friends Bunny and Cat.

"Have you lost anything today?" Hippo asks them.

Bunny and Cat look at each other. "Not that we know of," says Cat. "Why?"

"We found a dollar on the playground," Bear explains. "It's not yours, is it?"

Bear hopes the dollar does not belong to Bunny or Cat.

"That's a lot of money," says Bunny. "But I'm sure it's not mine."

"If a dollar of mine were missing," says Cat, "I would know right away!"

Bear and Hippo ask Cat and Bunny what they should do next.

"If I had a dollar," Bunny answers, "I would buy a snack before my dance lesson."

"I think you two are doing the right thing," says Cat. "You should keep asking around. If you can't find anyone who lost a dollar, then the dollar should belong to you."

Bear and Hippo cross over to the sandbox, where Pig and Mouse are digging in the sand.

"Have you lost anything today?" Bear asks them.

Pig and Mouse stop digging. "That depends," Mouse says playfully. "What did you find?"

"We found a dollar on the playground," Hippo explains. "It's not yours, is it?"

Hippo hopes the dollar does not belong to Pig or Mouse.

"You found a whole dollar?" says Pig. "What a stroke of luck!"

"We've been digging for treasure all day," says Mouse. "And all we've found so far is a bottle cap, a tin can, two pennies, and a rubber band."

Hippo and Bear ask Mouse and Pig what they should do next.

"Give the dollar to me," jokes Mouse. Bear and Hippo are sure they do not want to give it to her.

"You've done enough already," says Pig. "I think the dollar should belong to you now."

Friends Share

Bear thinks they have done all they could to find out who lost the dollar. Hippo disagrees and thinks they could do more.

Hippo and Bear have asked everyone at the playground except Puppy, who is sitting at the picnic table.

"Have you lost anything today?" Hippo asks him.

"I have been writing this letter to my great-granddog," says Puppy. "I haven't lost anything."

"We found a dollar on the playground," Bear explains. "It's not yours, is it?"

Bear hopes the dollar does not belong to Puppy.

"It's not my dollar," says Puppy. "But somebody must be missing it."

"We asked everybody here," says Bear. "Nobody is looking for it."

Bear and Hippo ask Puppy what they should do next.

"Why don't you put up a sign?" says Puppy. "Wait one day. If no one comes to claim the dollar, then it belongs to you."

Bear and Hippo wait at a picnic table all day. Many kids and their parents visit the playground that day.

Most of them pass by the sign on the fence. Some stop to read it. But nobody comes to them to ask about a missing dollar.

Hippo and Bear argue about what they should do next.

"Puppy said to wait one day," says Hippo.

"We've been here all day, Hippo!" Bear snaps.

"But the day is not over yet, Bear!" Hippo snaps back.

Bear and Hippo wait some more. They start making plans for spending the dollar.

"I think I'll buy a giant candy bar that will last a whole week!" Bear says.

"I'm saving up for a new football," says Hippo.

It is starting to get dark. Bear wants to get to the candy store before it closes. Hippo still thinks it is too soon to spend the money.

They both stare at the dollar, thinking of all the ways they could spend it.

"Let's wait until tomorrow," says Hippo. "Someone might come looking for it in the morning."

Bear remembers what Puppy said. "I guess you're right," he agrees at last. "I can wait until tomorrow."

Now Hippo and Bear just have to decide what to do with the dollar.

"I'll take it home," says Bear. "It will be safe with me."

"No way!" says Hippo. "You pass the candy store on your way home. The dollar is safer with me!"

Bear grabs one end of the dollar bill, and Hippo clutches the other. They tug it so hard, they almost tear it in half!

Hippo puts an end to their foolishness with a clever idea. "Why don't we hide it here until tomorrow?" he says.

"That's okay with me," Bear agrees.

To keep their treasure safe, they dig a little hole beside the picnic table. They bury the dollar there. Then they walk home together.

Both are still thinking about how to spend the money.

In the morning, Bear and Hippo arrive very early. At exactly the same time, they reach the spot where they left the dollar.

They stoop down to dig for their treasure. Hippo digs one side of the hole, and Bear digs the other. They dig deeper than they did before. They cannot find their dollar!

"I don't believe it!" they shout at exactly the same time. "It's gone!"

"You came back here last night to get it!" says Hippo.

"I did not!" Bear shouts. "You did!"

Puppy is just arriving at the playground. He hears his friends shouting at one another.

"What happened?" he asks.

"Hippo took my dollar!" says Bear, while Hippo says, "Bear took my dollar!"

Turtle comes over from the swing set. "Look what I found this morning!" he says happily. "A buried treasure!"

Turtle waves the dollar bill in the air.

"Hey!" Hippo and Bear both shout. "That's mine!"

Turtle thinks the dollar belongs to him. Bear and Hippo still think it belongs to them.

Puppy does not like to see his friends argue. He calmly tells them what he thinks about their problem.

"Only one person has the right to keep the whole dollar," says Puppy, "and that's whoever lost it in the first place. And if nobody claims it, I think the three of you should share it."

Turtle does not mind sharing his treasure. But Hippo and Bear mind a lot.

"Just a minute, guys," says Puppy. "You were sharing at the playground when you found the dollar. It's only right that you should be sharing when you spend it!"

Bear and Hippo know Puppy is right. The three friends agree to use the dollar to get something they all like.

"I guess it will be fun to share," Bear says at last.

Later that day, Hippo, Bear, and Turtle go to the ice cream parlor. They take turns sharing a sundae with three scoops of their favorite flavors.

The Secret Fort

Written by Brian Conway

Puppy and his friends have a special place to play, a place that is all their own. They have a secret playground, far off in the back of the forest.

At the foot of an old, hollow oak tree, Puppy and his friends have made a fort for themselves. They have been playing at the fort since they were all very little.

"We'll meet you at the fort," Puppy and Cat whisper to their friends after school. They hurry ahead through the quiet woods. There is not a path that leads to their private playground, but they all know the way.

No one ever goes there but them. The fort is a place where they can run and climb. They can be loud and silly. They all love playing games there all afternoon long.

The friends climb the old oak's knobby trunk. They swing from its sturdy branches. They leap across its thick, twisty roots. They play there almost every day. The secret fort is their favorite place to play.

The Secret Fort

The Secret Fort

The fort is their special playground. It is also their special meeting place. After a game of tag or hide-and-seek in the woods, Puppy and his friends huddle around the fort. They talk and tell jokes for hours.

The friends hide their treasures in their secret fort, too. Hippo keeps his lucky baseball tucked under the old oak's twisty roots. Puppy has a hiding place for a walking stick his uncle carved especially for him. Bear keeps more of his favorite treasures at the fort than he has at his house!

Today Bunny reaches under the wild roots, just to see what will turn up. She finds a little blanket wrapped inside a plastic bag.

"My blanket!" giggles Cat. "When I was a kitten, I never let go of it!"

"Remember how Cat used to wear it as a cape?" Puppy asks with a grin. Cat remembers, too. She puts it around her shoulders and pretends that she is Robin Hood.

The others cheer and clap for her. "You are the prettiest Robin Hood I know," Mouse giggles.

The next day at school, Ms. Hen tells her class the latest news in their town. Ms. Hen has learned about a plan to add a long walking path through the forest.

"The forest is the best place to learn about the wonders of nature," she tells her students. "Now all the families in town will have a chance to see the forest's beauty!"

With wide, worried eyes, Puppy and his friends look around the room. Puppy is the first to raise his hand.

"Just how long is this path?" he asks.

"Do you know which part of the forest it goes through?" adds Mouse.

Ms. Hen has a map of the new nature path at her desk. She shows it to the class.

"Well, it goes through every part of the woods, of course," she says, "from the park to the meadow, across the stream, and back into the trees."

Ms. Hen can see that the news has upset her students. She thought they would be happy about the new path.

Puppy and his friends cannot believe it! The path goes through every part of the woods, even through their own private playground!

They are all very upset, but Puppy is careful not to give away their secret place. "Why would anyone want to walk way out there?" he asks Ms. Hen. "There's nothing there but trees and leaves!"

"To see nature," says Ms. Hen. "The forest is an important part of our town."

Bunny is the saddest one of them all. Through tearful sobs she asks, "If the trees are so important, why are they cutting them down to build a silly path?"

Ms. Hen is pleased with Bunny's respect for nature. "Oh, Bunny, no," she says. "No trees will be cut down. The path goes around the trees. They will just put down some wood chips. It's really very easy. The path will be ready tomorrow!"

Puppy is starting to feel sick to his stomach. He does not want to share his special place!

By tomorrow, the woods will be busy with visitors. After school, Puppy and his friends make their way to their favorite place.

"This will be our last visit to the secret fort," Bunny sobs. "I'll miss it so much!"

"We all will," says Puppy sadly.

"We should get our things together," says Bear. "Our hiding place won't be hidden for long."

The friends dig through the old oak's roots, picking out all the treasures they had kept there. Each treasure reminds them of what fun they have had at their special place.

Cat uncovers a box of finds from their first rock hunt, and Hippo finds his lucky baseball.

But this treasure hunt also reminds them that their fun times at the secret fort are over. Cat sadly tucks her old blanket into her backpack. "I guess I won't be playing Robin Hood anymore," Cat says sadly. The others agree and slowly pack their treasures away, too.

The last thing Puppy finds among the roots is an old photo album. Last fall, Ms. Hen helped Puppy and his friends make a leaf book. The book is full of colorful leaves from different trees.

After they had picked up leaves that had fallen from their favorite trees in the forest, Ms. Hen showed them how to press each leaf into the album. Then they wrote down the type of tree the leaf came from. Puppy opens a page to show his friends.

"I know that leaf!" says Cat excitedly. "It's from the shady oak beside the brook."

Pig points out another one. "That's from the maple where we put our first tree swing!" he says.

Puppy takes his friends through the pages of the leaf book. Every tree brings back good memories.

The friends finish tidying up the old oak tree. They take one last look at their private playground in the woods before they turn around to walk slowly back to town.

At school the next day, Ms. Hen notices how sad her students seem. All morning long, they stare out the classroom window. They are thinking about their special fort and wondering who is playing there now.

Though she does not know why they are sad, Ms. Hen has an idea that she thinks will cheer them up.

"After lunch today," she announces, "we'll take a field trip!"

Her students like the sound of that!

"Wouldn't a nature walk through the woods be a fun thing to do today?" Ms. Hen asks.

Puppy and his friends droop down in their seats again until lunchtime. At lunch, Pig and Mouse say they do not want to go to the woods.

"It won't be the same," says Pig.

"I might cry in front of everybody!" says Mouse.

"It won't be the same," says Puppy, "but it still might be fun."

After lunch, Ms. Hen leads her class along the path.

The Secret Fort

Puppy and his friends are surprised to see that the path is very crowded. Some walk through the woods for exercise. Others stop to look at every plant and every tree. The younger kids run back and forth from the path and into the woods as they play.

Puppy and his friends are the only ones who are not having fun. The woods they know so well have changed.

"It seems like everyone in town is here," Pig whispers to his friends.

"Our secret playground looks like Main Street now!" Hippo complains.

"I wish everyone would just go back home," Bear sobs.

Ms. Hen is having a wonderful time. She points out the trees and flowers she wants her students to learn about. Ms. Hen does not understand why they are so sad.

Coming to their old oak tree, Ms. Hen calls to her students. "That big oak must be the oldest tree in the forest!" she says. "Why don't you play over there?"

Puppy and his friends gather around the old oak tree. Nobody says a word. They just sit there sadly, listening to all the strangers bustling along the path nearby.

"I liked our nature walks better before there was a path," says Bunny.

Just then a kitten wanders over to their fort in the tree. The curious little kitten is holding a big leaf.

"Excuse me," she says. "Do you know which tree this pretty leaf came from?"

Puppy and his friends all sit up straight. They have seen leaves like this one many times before. They know exactly where the leaf came from!

"That's an oak leaf," says Puppy. "It came from this tree we're sitting under."

Puppy remembers that he kept the leaf book in his backpack. He gets it out and shows the little kitten another big leaf from the same oak tree.

"What pretty leaves!" the kitten says. "I really love this book," she adds.

The Secret Fort

"None of the other oak trees in the forest have leaves that big," Puppy explains to the little kitten. "This is the oldest oak in the forest!"

"How do you know so much about nature?" asks the little kitten.

"We come here all the time," Bunny says.

"We know every tree in this part of the woods!" says Pig happily.

The kitten hears her mother calling. "I have to go," she says. "Will you show me more trees next time?"

Puppy and his friends are happy to share all they know about their favorite place in the woods. "Sure!" says Puppy. "These woods are for everyone to enjoy!"

"Bring some friends!" says Bear. "We'll show you the best places to play, too!"

"And if you ever want to know more about the trees here," Puppy says, as he tucks the leaf book back under the roots of the old oak, "this book will always be right here for you and your friends."

Silly Stunts

Written by Brian Conway

Puppy is playing in the sandbox with his friends and says, "Look what I made!"

Skunk and Turtle stop what they are doing to see Puppy's amazing sand castle.

"Wow!" says Turtle. "That looks great!"

Puppy is the best at making sand castles. Skunk looks down at the lump of sand he has shaped. Then he looks at the round mound of sand that Turtle is working on.

"Um, Puppy?" asks Skunk. "Can we help with your sand castle?"

Puppy is happy to share his skills with his friends. All of a sudden, a pink blur zips past the sandbox. Whoosh!

"What was that?" asks Turtle.

Whoosh! It zips by again, but this time the pink blur stops beside them.

"Hi, guys!" says Pig. "How do you like my new skates?"

Before they have a chance to answer, Pig is gone again, zooming his way around the playground.

Silly Stunts

Pig skates by a few times. He is a very speedy skater.

"How fast do you think I was going?" he asks.

Looking up from their sand castle, Puppy answers, "Very fast! We could hardly see you!"

Pig skates to the end of the playground and back.

"How fast was I going that time?" he asks.

By now, Turtle knows Pig is a fast skater. He thinks Pig is just showing off.

"We can't watch you skate now," he says politely.

Pig just shrugs and zips away to find his other friends. Bunny and Hippo are playing on the teeter-totter.

"How do you like my new skates?" Pig asks.

"Neat feet!" says Bunny. "How fast can you go?"

"Well," Pig brags, "I can skate very fast. Do you want to watch me?"

"Sure!" yells Hippo.

Bunny and Hippo giggle as they watch Pig skate in speedy circles around them.

"Just call me Pink Lightning," Pig cheers.

Pig is feeling a bit dizzy. But he still brags, "That was easy! I can go faster, you know."

"We know you can," Bunny laughs.

"Why don't you stop for a while?" says Hippo. "Bunny can show you her new dance steps."

Bunny learns a lot about balance in her dance classes. She can dance on one leg or spin on one toe. She moves very well.

She starts her routine, but Pig interrupts her. He does not want to sit around and watch Bunny now. He wants to show off his new skates! He thinks skating is more interesting than dancing.

"I can top that!" says Pig. "I can do it on skates!"

"Is that safe?" Bunny worries. "Please be careful, Pig."

Pig is not listening. First he skates backwards. Then he skates on one leg.

"Look at me!" Pig calls.

Bunny and Hippo cheer for Pig. They both think that he skates very well.

Pig wants to show the others his new skating tricks. He returns to the sandbox, where Puppy, Skunk, and Turtle are still playing.

"I have some new tricks," Pig tells them. "Are you ready for my Super Skating Show?"

"We know you're a good skater," says Turtle. "You don't have to show off for us."

Pig starts his skating routine anyway. He skates backwards, and he skates on one leg. He calls, "Look at me!"

Turtle does not want to watch, but Puppy and Skunk stop to see. Pig hops on one skate. Skunk cheers and claps for his friend.

"Look at me!" he calls again. Pig skates backward on one leg.

Skunk and Puppy like that trick. They ask him to do it again. Even Turtle watches this time. Pig is putting on a good show.

Soon Pig is all out of tricks.

His friends go back to building their sand castle. Pig's Super Skating Show is over.

That night Pig stays awake in bed, trying to think of new skating tricks that his friends will enjoy. Pig is not very good at making sand castles or dancing, but he is very good when he is wearing his new skates.

Hearing his friends clap for him makes him want to be the best. He wants to put on a spectacular skating show for his friends.

As Pig falls asleep, he dreams that he is a famous stunt skater. Lots of people come from all around to see Pig's amazing tricks.

In his dream, Pig is the star of the show. He skates through hoops and over ramps. He even jumps over a row of buses! He twists and spins, and the audience shouts for more. They are cheering for him!

The next morning, Pig has an idea for a great trick. He straps on his skates and spends the morning practicing jumps and spins.

Pig is ready to show his friends the new trick.

"Welcome to Pig's amazing show!" he announces. "I will now perform an amazing spinning trick called the Triple Tail Twister!"

Puppy, Skunk, and Turtle look up to see Pig's stunt. Pig steps back and skates ahead.

Picking up speed, Pig jumps into the air! He spins his body once, twice, and almost a third time before tumbling to the ground.

Turtle rushes to his side. Pig has scraped his leg.

Pig picks himself up. "It's nothing," he says. "I'm fine. Besides, the show must go on!"

"Are you sure that's a good idea?" asks Turtle. But Pig is not listening as he skates away to try the trick again.

Pig's second try is truly spectacular. He jumps and spins three times in the air, and this time he lands smoothly on his skates!

Skunk and Puppy clap and cheer. Even Turtle is amazed at the trick.

Pig skates to the playground. He wants all of his friends to see the new stunt.

Mouse and Bear are playing on the slide.

Pig announces, "Introducing the Spectacular Skating Pig! I will perform my best tricks for you!"

Pig shows them every trick he knows. He finishes his routine with the Triple Tail Twister. Mouse and Bear are amazed!

"More! More!" they shout.

Pig does not know any more tricks, but he does not want to disappoint his friends.

Pig thinks for a moment. The stunts in his dream were too hard. He could not do them now, not without a lot of practice. But Pig sees the slide and has an idea.

"I can skate down that slide and land on my feet!" he brags to his friends.

"Wait," says Bear, "that sounds dangerous!"

"I'd like to see it!" says Mouse.

"It will be my best trick yet," says Pig. "Call the others over to see!"

When Turtle and Puppy hear about Pig's plan, they rush to the slide. Pig is looking up at the tall slide. He has not climbed up its steep steps yet.

"Is it true?" Puppy asks. "You're going to skate down the slide?"

"Well, yes," answers Pig. He touches the sleek, slippery surface of the slide.

"That's just silly!" says Turtle. "You could get hurt doing a stunt like that!"

Bear and Bunny agree. Nobody wants to see their friend get hurt.

"But I promised to show you a new trick," says Pig bravely. "And the show must go on!"

"You don't have to show off for us," says Puppy. "We're your best friends!"

Turtle adds, "We don't need to see a lot of silly stunts. We would rather see our friend in one piece!"

Pig is glad his friends came to stop him. "I was really scared to do that trick," he admits. "I guess it was foolish of me to brag like that."

"You're the best skater we know!" says Turtle.

The others agree with him.

"Everyone is good at something," Bunny adds. "Puppy is the best at sand castles, and I'm the best at dancing."

"But we don't have to put on a show to prove it," adds Puppy.

"Claps and cheers are nice," says Bunny, "but mostly we just like to share our best skills with our friends!"

Pig promises he will be more careful. He does not want to hurt himself while he skates.

"But I have one more trick to show you!" Pig says. "It's an amazing stunt my best friends taught me."

Pig sits down and takes off his skates. He climbs up the slide and slides down, simply and safely. His friends clap and cheer more than ever.

Helping Out

Written by Amy Adair

It is a beautiful day. The sun is shining, and Puppy and his friends enjoy their walk to school.

Bunny dances ahead of the group, showing Cat and Mouse a new ballet step.

Bear and Puppy talk about a new game they want to play at recess. All of a sudden, Bunny stops dancing and quietly falls into step with Puppy.

"What's wrong?" Puppy asks Bunny. Bunny does not say anything, she just frowns and points at the house they are passing.

Puppy shivers as they all hurry past the scary house. The grass looks like it has not been mowed in weeks. There are no flowers.

Cat whispers, "This house looks so awful. It looks so scary." Mouse agrees, and skips beside her friends just to keep up with them.

In no time at all, the friends can see the familiar red schoolhouse. They all breathe a sigh of relief.

"Who do you think lives there?" Bunny asks, as she gracefully twirls around.

"I don't know," Mouse answers.

"I bet no one lives there," Bear says.

"I think you're right, Bear," Puppy says. "And I bet that house will be torn down."

They all agree with Puppy.

Then Bear and Puppy begin to talk about recess again. Bear can hardly wait to teach Puppy a new game.

Mouse tells Bunny that the morning is her favorite part of the day because Ms. Hen always reads them a story.

Bunny giggles and does a final dance move up the school steps.

They have all forgotten about the scary house and hurry to their seats to listen to Ms. Hen's morning story.

"Good morning!" Ms. Hen says to her cheerful students.

"Good morning, Ms. Hen," they all say in chorus.

Puppy and his friends settle down in their seats.

"Today," Ms. Hen says, "we're going to read a story about helping people in need."

Bunny smiles. She loves to help people, so she pays extra-close attention to today's story.

Ms. Hen opens up a big book and stands in front of the class. She reads about how lending a helping hand can brighten someone's day.

Ms. Hen turns the page and reads about two friends named Kitten and Tiger. In the story, Kitten lost her favorite kite in a tree and could not reach it to get it down. Kitten was very sad and even started to cry. She thought she had lost her kite forever.

Tiger did not like to see Kitten so sad. Since he was so much taller, he could easily reach her kite.

"Helping makes everyone feel better," Ms. Hen says. After Ms. Hen finishes the story, Bunny quickly raises her hand and asks if Ms. Hen knows anyone that needs help.

Ms. Hen smiles at Bunny. "Yes," Ms. Hen says, "I know somebody who needs help."

Helping Out

"I want to help, too," Puppy says.

"So do I," says Bear.

"Me too," says Cat.

"Don't forget about me," says Mouse.

Ms. Hen tells the class about Ms. Panda. She needs some help taking care of her lawn and planting her flowers. Ms. Hen adds that Ms. Panda loves to see happy faces.

Everyone cheers and begins talking about how they will help Ms. Panda.

"When can we go to her house to help?" Bear wonders.

"Well, I suppose I could show you where she lives right after school," Ms. Hen says.

Ms. Hen is very proud of all her students. She knows how much it will mean to Ms. Panda to have somebody help her. Ms. Hen also knows that seeing young students will brighten Ms. Panda's whole day.

Bunny and Mouse can hardly wait for school to be over. Puppy and Bear spend recess talking about helping Ms. Panda instead of playing their new game.

As soon as the bell rings, Ms. Hen leads the friends to Ms. Panda's house.

Puppy can hardly believe his eyes when Ms. Hen stops in front of the scary house that they passed on their way to school this morning. "This can't be where Ms. Panda lives!" Bunny says.

Before anyone can answer, Ms. Panda opens the front door and smiles. Somehow the house does not look so scary now. Ms. Hen waves to Ms. Panda and tells her students that she will see them tomorrow at school.

The friends quickly get to work. Puppy and Bear rake the leaves. Cat and Bunny water the plants.

As usual, Mouse is too small to help. She sadly sits on the porch and watches her friends.

Mouse feels very sad and lonely. She wishes she could do something to help Ms. Panda, too.

Then Mouse sees that Ms. Panda is sitting on the porch by herself, too. At the same time, Ms. Panda notices how sad Mouse is and gets an idea.

Helping Out

Helping Out

"Will you please help me read this book?" Ms. Panda kindly asks Mouse. Ms. Panda taps the cover of the book that is resting on her lap.

Mouse is shy at first because there are some words that she does not know how to pronounce. Ms. Panda tells her that she will help her sound out all the hard words.

Mouse sits on Ms. Panda's lap and begins to read. She stumbles over some words, but Ms. Panda gently helps her sound them out.

Mouse loves reading to Ms. Panda, and Ms. Panda loves listening to Mouse read. The two are instant friends!

Before long, Ms. Panda's yard looks beautiful and Mouse is done reading the book.

"Thank you for reading that story to me," Ms. Panda whispers to Mouse.

Mouse smiles at her new friend.

Ms. Panda looks at all the work Puppy, Bear, Cat, and Bunny did. She is truly amazed! Her big yard looks so neat and clean!

Puppy says he wants to come back next week to take care of her lawn again. Bear says he will come back and help, too.

Bunny and Cat tell Ms. Panda how much they would like to take care of her plants.

"I love planting flowers," Cat says.

"And I love watering them," Bunny adds. Cat and Bunny make a very good team.

Mouse whispers that she would like to come back and read to Ms. Panda.

Ms. Panda smiles at all of her new friends and says, "You are all welcome to come back anytime you want." Ms. Panda loves all of her little helpers.

The friends walk home together and talk about how much they liked helping Ms. Panda. They can hardly wait to go back and help her again.

Mouse is very quiet because she thinks that she did not help Ms. Panda at all. She wishes she could be big like the rest of her friends.

Helping Out

The next day the friends walk to school together. They can't wait to get to Ms. Panda's house.

This time when they walk past the house, they wave to Ms. Panda. She sits happily on the porch waiting for her helping friends.

She waves for them to come up and see her. She hands Cat, Bear, and Puppy a bag full of cookies!

"Thank you for helping me yesterday," she says to her little friends.

"We really like helping you, Ms. Panda," Puppy says.

"It was sure nice meeting you," Ms. Panda says. She hands Bunny a bag of cookies, too. Bunny smiles at Ms. Panda. Bunny loved helping Ms. Panda.

Mouse is the last one to get her cookies. "Thank you for helping me," Ms. Panda says to Mouse and gently pats her on the head.

Mouse smiles at Ms. Panda, but she wishes she could have helped clean the yard.

Ms. Panda tells them to hurry along to school so they will not be late.

The friends race to school and can hardly wait to tell Ms. Hen how much they loved helping Ms. Panda.

Ms. Hen greets them at the schoolhouse door. Everyone starts talking at once.

Puppy says he loved taking care of Ms. Panda's lawn. He also tells Ms. Hen that helping someone made him feel very good. He cannot wait to go back.

Bear agrees, and says that he wants to help Ms. Panda with her yard every week.

Bunny and Cat explain how they planted new flowers for Ms. Panda. They tell Ms. Hen that they are going back to help her water them next week.

Mouse is very quiet. She thinks that no one notices that she is there. She also thinks that no one even noticed her yesterday afternoon at Ms. Panda's house.

All the students file into the school except Mouse and Ms. Hen.

"So how did you like helping Ms. Panda?" Ms. Hen asks Mouse quietly.

"I didn't do anything to help. I'm too small," Mouse answers. She says that while the others were working very hard in the yard, she only read a story to Ms. Panda.

Ms. Hen notices that Mouse is holding a brown paper bag, and she asks what is inside.

Mouse tells Ms. Hen that Ms. Panda gave them all cookies this morning to thank them for helping her. Mouse opens the bag to show Ms. Hen and finds a note. It reads:

Dear Mouse,

    You were the biggest help of all yesterday. Sometimes my old eyes won't let me read very long anymore. You have such a lovely reading voice. Please come back and read to me again. You truly brightened my day.

Love,
Ms. Panda

Imagination

Written by Brian Conway

It is a rainy day outside, so Puppy invites Hippo over to his house. They empty out everything in Puppy's toy box, looking for something fun to play.

Puppy tosses aside his ball and old picture books. He is not in the mood to play with them today. Puppy does not even bother to put the toys away.

Hippo stares out the window. He wishes the rain would stop so they could go outside and play.

"I'm bored," says Hippo. "What should we do now?"

"I don't know," says Puppy. "I wish we could go outside to play."

Hippo finds a board game under the couch.

"Let's play this," he suggests. "Do you want to be the blue piece or the purple piece?"

"Boring!" says Puppy. "Why do you think they call them 'bored' games, anyway?"

"Rainy days are the worst," Hippo sighs. "There's nothing to do but sit around and stare!"

Imagination

Staring at the walls and the floor, Hippo looks for something fun in Puppy's playroom. Nothing looks fun. Hippo tries to think of something for them to do.

"I have an idea!" says Hippo. "We played with everything here already, so let's play with something that's not here!"

"What are you talking about, silly?" Puppy giggles.

"We can pretend!" says Hippo.

He thinks of a new game. Hippo calls it Guess Who. Hippo thinks of somebody and pretends to be that person. Puppy must guess the pretend person.

Hippo sits down on the floor. He moves his foot and his arms. He makes a funny rumbling sound.

"Vrrroom," he says. "Guess who I am? Vrrroom!"

"Are you a cement mixer?" Puppy chuckles.

Hippo laughs, too. "Guess again," he says, turning an imaginary steering wheel. "Errr! Vrrroom!"

"I know!" says Puppy. "You're a race car driver!"

Hippo claps for Puppy. "Yes!" Hippo says.

Puppy makes up another imagination game. He calls it Guess What. In this game, Puppy pretends to see something in the room, and he gives Hippo a few hints about what he is pretending to see.

"I think I'll climb up it and pick a red apple," Puppy pretends.

Hippo guesses right away. "A tree!" he calls out.

Puppy starts another game of Guess What.

"Now look at this," Puppy says, pointing to the empty floor. "It's round and has three holes in the side." Puppy pretends to pick something up. "Ooo, it's so heavy," he says laughing.

He pretends to roll it across the floor. Then Puppy pretends to watch it roll away. Puppy laughs and makes a big crashing sound!

Hippo is laughing hard, too. He is almost laughing too hard to guess. "I think it's a bowling ball!" he guesses at last. Hippo guesses right!

"This is so much fun!" Puppy says.

In the middle of their game Puppy's doorbell rings.

Cat, Bear, and Turtle are standing outside in the rain. Puppy invites them in.

"We were at Cat's house," says Bear, "but there was nothing to do there."

"We were so bored," Turtle says.

"So we came over to see if you were having any fun!" Cat adds.

Hippo tells them they were very bored all day, too.

"Then we made up some new games!" says Puppy. "They're lots of fun, and you don't need any toys to play!"

"Guess what I'm doing!" Hippo calls out. He pretends to hold a watering can, which he pretends to pour all over the table. Puppy cannot stop giggling long enough to explain the game to his confused friends.

"What's he doing?" asks Turtle.

"He's watering a pretend flower!" says Puppy.

Puppy and Hippo laugh. Cat, Bear, and Turtle just look at each other. They do not understand what is so funny.

Puppy tells his other friends how to play their new imagination games. "You have to use your imaginations," he says. "You can pretend to be someone. That is Guess Who! It's fun!"

"Or you can pretend to see something," says Hippo. "That is Guess What."

Puppy quickly flips off the lights. "Let's play Guess Where!" he says. "Imagine you are in a dark, underground place. Now tell me what you see."

Cat is catching on. "Eek! I see a bat!" she shrieks.

"I just walked through a spiderweb!" says Bear. "Where is my flashlight?"

"I'm almost too tall," Hippo adds.

Turtle still does not see what his friends are pretending to see. He flips on the light. "You were pretending to be inside a dark cave, right?" he guesses. "But it still looks like Puppy's playroom to me!"

"You won!" Puppy tells Turtle. "Now it's your turn to make up a pretend place!"

"Maybe I'll stay for one game," Turtle says. "Now, let me think."

Turtle thinks for a long time. Soon he sits on the floor and thinks some more.

"Okay," he says, "guess where I am?"

"Are you at school?" Hippo jokes. Turtle slowly shakes his head.

"You look bored," says Puppy. "Are you watching a dumb movie?"

"Guess again," Turtle says with a grin.

"That's a tough one," says Bear. "We give up."

Turtle looks around and frowns again. "I imagined it's raining outside," he says, "and we're all stuck inside Puppy's house!"

Puppy and the others laugh out loud.

"You're funny, Turtle," says Puppy. "And you have a great imagination! Now try it again."

"Think of any place at all," says Hippo, "and we'll be there with you."

Turtle says he will play another game of Guess Where. Turtle thinks of a wonderful place for this game. "We're in a big stone building with tall walls all around it," he says smiling.

Nobody can guess where Turtle is imagining.

Pointing at Puppy, he says, "I see a brave knight on horseback!"

Walking over to Cat and Bear, Turtle adds, "And you must be the lovely princess and her father, the king."

Hippo starts laughing! "It's a castle, right?" he calls out.

Turtle is having too much fun pretending. He sneaks up on Hippo. "What's this?" he says, poking Hippo's nose. "Oh, dear! A giant, flying, fire-breathing dragon!"

"Run away!" the others shout.

The friends are having so much fun, they decide to keep playing Turtle's game of Guess Where. It is the best game all day! Puppy and Turtle even make a castle out of a big empty box.

Puppy has a great idea. "Let's play Guess Who, Guess What, and Guess Where all at the same time!" he suggests. "We'll put on a play!"

"We'll need costumes!" says Cat. She and Bear make hats for everybody.

Turtle wants to be the court jester in their play. He uses a paper bag to make a silly shirt.

Puppy and Hippo talk about what kinds of things they would see around a real castle.

"My horse is in the stable," says Knight Puppy, who rushes to find a broom in the closet.

Pretending to be a flying dragon, Hippo makes some pointy teeth and wide wings for himself.

"A dragon has to have a spooky lair," Hippo says. He makes a place for a dragon to hide.

Puppy's playroom is starting to look like a stage. Turtle's castle game is getting more and more real. The friends are almost ready to begin their play.

Puppy and his friends make up their play as they go along. Their pretending gets very silly sometimes. Once in a while, Turtle the Jester makes them giggle so much that they have to stop.

But they are having a wonderful afternoon, and their play feels very real to them. Right there in Puppy's playroom, the friends are on an exciting adventure.

"The evil dragon has captured my daughter!" King Bear announces at the castle.

Sir Puppy rides up on his pretend horse. "I will save Princess Cat!" he says.

"Jester!" calls King Bear. "Show Sir Puppy the way to the dragon's lair!"

Turtle leads the way to Hippo's hideout. They hear Princess Cat crying for help. Suddenly the dragon leaves its lair. It spreads its wings and charges Sir Puppy!

"Um, boo!" says Hippo softly. The others cannot stop laughing!

"You are not a very scary dragon!" Turtle chuckles.

"Okay," says Hippo, "then let's pretend I'm breathing fire at you!"

Turtle runs for cover, while brave Sir Puppy comes face-to-face with the dragon.

Sir Puppy wins his battle with the fire-breathing dragon! He rescues Princess Cat from the dragon's spooky lair. King Bear gives Sir Puppy a fine new horse to ride. All the friends cheer.

"That was fun!" says Turtle when their play is over. "Maybe rainy days aren't so bad after all!"

"Wait!" says Puppy. "Our play is not over yet!"

"We all have to take a bow!" says Hippo. "Guess why!"

"I know!" says Cat. "Our play was a big hit, and all the pretend people in our pretend audience loved it!"

"That's right!" says Hippo, pointing to an empty wall near their stage. "They're clapping for us right now!"

"Well, imagine that!" says Turtle, turning to the wall to take a bow.